Viable

Wendy Zuccarello

Published by Wendy Zuccarello, 2023.

This is a work of fiction. Similarities to real people, places, or events are entirely coincidental.

VIABLE

First edition. February 1, 2023.

Copyright © 2023 Wendy Zuccarello.

ISBN: 979-8227599117

Written by Wendy Zuccarello.

Table of Contents

To my husband, Anthony.

Thank you for always supporting my crazy ideas and for making me feel like I can conquer the world.

My name is Cassidy Daniels. I am twenty-four years old. I am five foot six with dirty blonde hair and hazel eyes. I weigh... well, you don't need to know that.

At this point in time, those are about the only "normal" things that I can tell you about myself.

I can tell you that I used to be a graduate student at the University of Wisconsin. I was planning on becoming a Child Therapist. I had a loving mother and father who raised me to be a responsible, caring young woman. I had an older brother, Austin, who was also my best friend. He was a Marine. We lived in a rural neighborhood, outside of Madison, Wisconsin. We had a beautiful two-story colonial home complete with the white picket fence.

I had a completely wonderful, normal life.

Had, being the keyword.

But then the world changed in a matter of days. Life changed.

The first wave hit sometime in late June of 2035. I went to bed, and everything was normal. But I woke up to a nightmare. My completely healthy, vibrant mother had died in her sleep, for no apparent reason. It happens sometimes, we knew that. Sometimes people die unexpectedly – brain aneurysm or whatever. But they couldn't explain it. She just died.

The weird thing was that she wasn't the only one. The news told us that thousands upon thousands of women had also passed, for no apparent reason.

Reports came in from all over the world that almost half of the world's female population had died. Half. Women of all ages, races, and nationalities died. It didn't seem to have any type of pattern.

And no one knew why.

Life tried to continue as normally as possible. Funeral homes were swamped with people trying to bury their loved ones. Cemeteries were overrun, quickly running out of space. It seemed that the entire country was in mourning.

Our world's leaders were trying to reassure those of us who remained that they were doing everything they could to figure out what happened. Weeks passed, and life was doing everything it could to return to normal. People went back to work. Life goes on, right?

And that's when the second wave hit, and so many more women were dead.

All hell broke loose. Riots, looting, violence, murders. You name it, we had it. They declared Martial Law in the entire country. The entire country. Who knows what was going on in the rest of the world? But there weren't enough people to enforce it. The police force and National Guard took major hits with the losses. A lot of the remaining soldiers and officers were more focused on protecting their families, that they never reported for duty. And who could blame them.

We lost all forms of communication. No TV, no internet, no phones. With no news, no one knew what to do.

Rumors began to spread about government facilities that were being set up to protect people. If you were a surviving female, you could go to one of the facilities for sanctuary. They even let you bring your family. We knew of a few people who went, looking for safety. We never heard from them again.

As time went on, there were groups that began hunting females. Rumor was if you turned a viable female into the facilities, you were rewarded with food and supplies. These hunters invaded homes, chased people down, and killed. Just to get females.

I lost everything. And now, I'm on my own.

So, the following is my story. I want to write everything down, just in case. I don't know if I will make it. I have no idea what the future holds for me. What I do know, is that I have to keep moving or they will find me.

My name is Cassidy Daniels.

And this is the story of how I was declared a viable female and survived the new normal.

1

Captured

The first thing I feel when I come to is a throbbing headache. I try not to make a move or change my breathing. I don't want them to know that I am awake yet. I need to try and assess my situation first. I can feel that my hands and feet are secured to whatever type of table I am laying on and I have a catheter in my right arm. There are some bright lights on, I can tell even though I haven't opened my eyes yet. I can hear mumbling, talking to my right. They must be on the other side of a wall or door though because I can't make out what they are saying, or how many there are.

Oh yeah. I am naked, too. Just great.

I do know one thing for sure. I am in serious trouble.

They caught me off guard. I thought I was pretty safe at the cabin that I had been staying at for the last few weeks, but I guess I was wrong. I had gone hunting, and when I came back, I could feel something was off before I even walked in the door.

I left my kills on the back porch and snuck in through the side door. Someone had been there, and everything was a mess. But the real clue that I wasn't alone was the massive pain on the back of my head when they knocked me out.

Now, here I am in one of their facilities. I have heard rumors about these places, which is why I was completely avoiding them. I didn't think I was anywhere near one at the cabin. I must have slipped and made a mistake, somehow alerting them to my presence.

I had been hiding out at a vacant cabin that I had found in the forests of North Carolina. It looked like no one had been there for a long time so I thought I would be safe. I was so careful about lighting fires and going outside.

There are always people out hunting for women, looking for the rewards for a capture. From what I have heard, if you bring in a viable female, you are rewarded generously with food and supplies.

Viable female. Yeah, that's what they call us.

"I know you are awake," someone says, a male. He sounds like a smoker from his scratchy voice.

I blink open my eyes, adjusting to the bright lights shining down on me. I look to my left and see the man. He looks to be in his fifties. He's really short, wearing glasses and a white lab coat. His balding head and big nose do nothing to distract from the giant belly he has. Makes me think that if I got the chance, I wouldn't have any problems out running him.

The room is completely white. No windows, only one door. What look like medical machines are lined up all along the walls. The beeping of what I assume is a heart monitor alerts this man to my increased heart rate.

I take a deep breath, trying to calm myself. I think of what Austin, my brother would say.

"You have to be able to control your breathing and facial expressions in any situation. You don't want your enemies to know what you are thinking or feeling."

"Who are you?" I ask, my voice is rough from just waking up.

"That's not really important right now," he says, smirking, making his way over to a computer in the corner.

"Silly me. I guess I wasn't thinking. You're right. It's not important for me to know who you are. I mean, you only have me tied to a table, naked," I say with sass.

My mother used to always tell me that I was born with a smart mouth. That I came out sassing her. My brother, on the other hand, always told me that my mouth was going to get me killed one day. Guess old habits are hard to break.

"I would watch your tone, young lady. You have no idea whom you are dealing with," he warns.

"Hence, why I asked who you are," I say. I can't help it; the wise-ass comments keep coming out. There is no stopping them.

"Hmm. You are going to be trouble, aren't you?" he says with a frown. "They aren't going to like that."

"Well, I do aim to please," I say while smiling.

"What's your name?" he asks.

"Goldilocks. By the way, have you seen my three bears anywhere?" I say back to him, looking around like I'm trying to actually find my three bears.

He does not look amused.

"I will ask you one more time. And if you do not cooperate, I will be forced to use other means of getting information. Means, my dear, that you will not enjoy," he says, running his eyes up and down my body.

I am trying to figure out if he is bluffing. I am now noticing a slight accent on him, not able to identify what type. He doesn't seem like a sadistic man, just rude.

"Name," he says again, irritated with me.

I don't say anything right away, I want to see what he will do.

"Fine," he says, and stomps out of the room.

I take the opportunity to really take in my surroundings. I look for anything that might help me get out of these bindings. They are tight, and they don't have any give. There is a tray sitting off to the side with some instruments on it. Maybe I could use one of those to loosen the bindings. I struggle to free something, anything. A foot, a hand. But I think I am just making the ropes tighter.

The door opens again and Mister Grumpy walks in followed by a younger man pushing a tray that has on it, an assortment of syringes. The younger man leaves the tray right next to my head and then walks out, leaving me alone with Mister Grumpy again.

He comes over to the tray and runs his hand back and forth over the syringes, as if he is having trouble deciding something.

"What are those?" I ask, my curiosity getting the better of me.

He chuckles.

"These, my dear, are incentive," he picks one up and flicks it a couple of times, causing bubbles to raise up in the dark liquid.

He grabs the tube that is coming out of my arm and sticks the needle in the port. Before he does anything, he looks into my eyes and smiles. It's definitely not meant to be a smile of reassurance. Not even close. Not with the way his eyes are squinted. This is a sadistic smile as if he is going to enjoy what happens. I guess I was wrong about my assumption. He is not a nice man.

He pushes just slightly on the syringe so that a little bit of the dark liquid goes into my catheter.

And then, there is pain.

I have never felt pain like this before in my life. An immense burning sensation travels up my arm and through my body. I feel like I am on fire. As much as I try to avoid it, I can't help it. I scream. I scream and thrash for some type of relief. I just want it to stop. I hear the man chuckling some more which only fuels my hatred for him and my situation. I continue to scream and cry. Everything is on fire, and I feel like I am dying. I think just about every single curse word that I know, and probably some new ones comes out of my mouth.

After what seems like hours, but was probably only minutes, the burning starts to ebb. I have no idea how long it lasted. It could have been seconds or days. I just know that I don't ever want to feel that again.

He chuckles again. I now have a new least favorite sound.

"Now, let's try this again. What is your name?" grumpy asks me.

I am still panting from the pain, but I manage to get out my name.

"Cassidy Daniels," I say angrily, panting from the exertion.

"Ah, so we are going to be more cooperative now, are we? I told you I had ways of making you talk," he says and smirks.

"You're going to pay for that someday," I growl.

"I assure you, I am not," he says while smiling.

He grabs another syringe and flicks it.

"Age?" he asks, sticking the new needle into the port.

I glare at him.

"This is going to take a long time if you keep needing encouragement. I can only give you so much each day without killing you. And we both know that I don't have the option of killing you."

"Twenty-four," I say begrudgingly.

"Thank you," he says as he pushes the plunger slightly, injecting a different liquid into my vein. This one is red, and it is most definitely different.

There is no fire this time, only agony. I can't really describe it other than to say it feels as if my bones are breaking and all my insides are being torn out of my body. No movement, no position makes it any better. Again, I scream, my throat beginning to get sore, but I have no choice. I couldn't keep quiet no matter how hard I tried.

When it starts to dull, I find my voice. "Why... did... you... do... that, you dick! I... answered your... question," I manage to get out between pants.

"Just as a reminder of what will happen if you don't play nice," he says.

The questions keep coming. And in between every few questions, he injects a little more of something from his arsenal. I have never known pain like this before. I lived a normal life. Who in their right mind would ever expect to be tortured like this?

"Where are you from?" he asks.

"Wisconsin."

"Are you alone?"

"Yes."

"Were you always alone?"

I don't want to tell him about Austin, but I also don't want any more encouragement.

"I was with my brother for a while, but I haven't seen him in a long time," I say, trying not to cry.

Austin, my brother, was five years older than me. He was the classic all-American boy. Tall, lean, muscular, with blonde hair and hazel eyes. We had the same eyes. He was my best friend. And now, I have no idea where he is.

"How did you get separated?" he asks.

I give him a brief description, trying not to divulge too much information.

"What happened to your mother?"

"She died."

"How and when?"

I pause.

"You know how," I say angrily, a tear running down my cheek.

"Explain, please," he says.

"I don't want to talk about it," I say hatefully.

"It really doesn't matter what you want, Miss Daniels. Now answer the question before I make you," he says, holding up another syringe.

It's been a while since I thought about it. It's such a painful memory.

"You know exactly what happened! It's the same thing that happened to everyone else. One day she was fine, the next, she was gone."

"First wave or second wave?" he asks.

I glare at him, trying to use the force to smash his head. I guess my Jedi skills haven't fully developed yet.

"First wave. Second wave. What does it matter? She's dead," I pan.

"It actually matters a great deal, my young friend."

That makes no sense. If all these women died for no reason, around the same time, what's the difference if it was immediately or weeks later? Like the stupid cat, my curiosity gets the better of me.

"I don't understand. Why?"

"That's not important right now. Just answer the question," he says.

I hesitate, thinking about what he said. If there is a difference between the first and second wave... if they know that, then maybe they know what is going on.

I must hesitate too long because I look up in time to see him injecting something new.

I scream. "First wave! First wave! Stop doing that, you asshole! They are all gone! All of them. First wave. Second wave. It doesn't matter. Whatever is happening, happened to everyone," I scream at him.

"Well, now, Miss Daniels, it didn't happen to *everyone* n*ow,* did it? That's why you are here. To help us figure this thing out," he says.

"So, I'm here for you to experiment on?"

"Well, not experiment on, per se. You are just going to willingly provide us with some blood and other samples, then we will complete our physical exam. If all checks out, you will enter the breeding program that we have set up."

"Breeding program? What the hell are you talking about?"

I am instantly filled with fear. Everyone has heard about the breeding programs. Up until now, I had no idea that they were real. I find myself panicking. My breathing picks up, along with my heart rate. The heart monitor gets louder.

"Now, now, Miss Daniels. You'd better calm down or I will be forced to use some more liquid encouragement," he says in warning.

He turns around, giving me his back. I can hear him typing away on his computer. I have never felt this exposed before. They are going to do things to me that I am sure I will never forget. Not that I will forget the torture, but I would hope that I will eventually be able to not remember how bad... never mind. I know I will never forget how those injections felt. My anger is at a new level now.

"Why are you doing this to me? Are you just a sadistic freak?" I say accusingly at him.

"Miss Daniels, do you know just how many we lost to this mysterious illness? Do you? Seventy-five percent. Take a moment and think about that." He pauses for effect. "That's a real number, a very big number. That is a lot of females, Miss Daniels. And we have yet to identify the issue. No one has been able to figure out why we lost three-quarters of the women on the planet in a matter of weeks. And then add the lives lost to the riots that ensued after the fact, and the human population has suffered massive losses. So yes, we are in survival mode. Those of us who remain, have the responsibility of ensuring that we survive. These facilities were set up to research the problem and develop a solution. I'm not sure if you are aware, but even babies born now are dying. Doesn't matter if the mother is immune for whatever reason, we are losing more and more each day. That is why we are researching not only the surviving women but also the men, to determine which couples have the best chance of providing us with viable infants. Infants, that will eventually be able to produce their own viable offspring."

I must look stunned because he laughs.

"Had I known the way to shut you up was to tell you how dire our situation is, I would have led with that," he laughs. "Now just a few more questions."

He continues firing off question after question. I'm too shocked to argue at this point. So, I just answer. Question, answer. Question, answer. Question, answer. He at least gives me a break from the injections.

When he finally finishes, a team of nurses and doctors comes in and start the physical exam he was talking about. They take blood, x-rays, nasal swabs... other swabs. They perform test after test after test and it goes on for hours and hours. I feel like a guinea pig. I am poked and prodded so much that I begin to just ache.

After they finish, I am transferred to a different room where they finally leave me alone. This room is also all white, but there is absolutely no furniture. No bed, no chairs. Nothing. Just four walls and a door. I am so exhausted, from the torture, from the exams, that I end up just curling up on the floor and passing out.

2

Preparations

"What are you doing?"

"What does it look like I'm doing? I'm washing dishes," I say.

Austin, my brother, comes up behind me and takes the gun from my hand.

"You can't fire the gun out here. Someone will hear it," he says, the disappointment clear in his voice.

"How else are we going to find something to eat?" I ask, my hands on my hips.

He shakes his head, frustrated with me yet again.

"Did you not pay any attention to anything that I have taught you?" he asks, ruffling the hair on the top of my head.

"Don't do that. You know I hate it," I say in a whine.

"Yeah. That's why I do it, kid." He laughs and picks up his bag.

"Come on. We have to get moving. We've already been here too long," Austin says.

"Now where are we going?" I ask.

"The same place we've been trying to get to since we left home," he says. "We have to find Cooper's cabin. I know he will be there. And between the two of us, maybe we can keep you safe."

"I don't even know Cooper. How am I supposed to trust him?" I ask, annoyed with him.

"Cass, I've told you a thousand times. Coop is like my brother. We were in basic training together and we served overseas together for years. I know him better than I know myself at this point. He is the only other person on *this planet that I trust to take care of you. If Dad were here, he would say the same thing."*

We've been traveling on foot for months. We started out in the car, but there ended up being too many roadblocks, checking for women. I would hide in the trunk at first, but then they started searching the cars. It became too dangerous to be on the roads. So, we grabbed everything that we could carry and took off on foot, trying to get to Cooper's cabin in the woods. It is in North Carolina apparently. Somewhere off the grid.

Austin and Cooper were in the Marines together before all of this happened. And on each and every leave that he had; Austin "trained" me. He always said that he wanted me to be able to take care of myself should something happen. He taught me survival skills, hunting, weapons. You name it, he taught me.

Who would have ever thought that I would need the training, unfortunately, things happen.

Now, here we are, hiking across the country, looking for his friend.

I hear a noise up ahead of us. Sounds like wildlife running through the brush so I don't think much of it. When I hear it a second time, I stop dead.

"Austin, did you hear that?" I ask.

He doesn't get the chance to answer because a shot rings out and he drops to the ground.

"No!" I scream and drop to the ground beside him. Blood is pouring from the wound on his shoulder.

"Damn it," he says with a growl. He is holding his shoulder, cursing in pain.

"Cassidy, look at me," he says, trying to get my attention. He is immediately in soldier mode.

My focus is on attending to his wound. I am tearing through my pack, looking for my first aid supplies when he grabs my hands.

"Cass!"

"What?" I ask between tears.

"You need to go. They will be here in a few minutes. That shot didn't come from too far away. You can't let them get you."

"No way," I say. "I am not leaving you!"

"You have to, Cass," he says, putting his hand up and pushing some of my hair behind my ear. "I love you, kid. I love you so damn much. Go. Go and find Cooper. He will take care of you. Don't trust anyone but him. And use what I taught you. You'll be fine, kid," he says, a tear running down his cheek.

"Austin, I won't leave you. I can't," I say, barely forming words due to the sobs.

"Go, Cass. I'll find you again, I promise."

He pushes up off the ground and runs toward the people who shot him.

"No!"

I feel someone holding me down, which doesn't make sense, because it was just the two of us.

"Wake up," the timid voice says. "It's just a dream. You have to wake up."

Wake up? Wait a minute. I blink my eyes, now realizing where I am. I must have fallen asleep and dreamed about when Austin and I got separated. That was months ago. I don't even know if he is even still alive. All the questioning yesterday must have stirred up memories.

I start to cry. Austin was all that I had. We lost our mom back when all of this first started. Dad was killed a week later in a struggle at our house. They were going door to door, looking for surviving women, and he wouldn't let them in the house. I was hiding in the attic while Austin and Dad talked to them. They insisted on coming in and began to push my dad back. The struggle got violent, and the invaders shot my dad in the head. Austin was able to fight them off, but the damage had already been done. Dad was gone.

So, in a matter of weeks, we lost both of our parents.

Coming upon the realization that everyone is after you is not a good feeling. We knew we had to get out of there. We had to run.

We packed everything we could carry, mostly supplies for survival, and left. I did manage to grab a few sentimental items while Austin wasn't looking. A photo of my parents, some photos of Austin and me growing up, my journal. I grabbed one last thing and shoved it in my bag. Austin and I jumped into his Jeep and took off.

"Are you awake now?" the person asks, bringing me back to reality.

I blink, trying to clear my eyes, and my head for that matter, and look up into the face of a young girl. She looks to be about fifteen or sixteen years old. And she looks like she wants to be anywhere but here. Her eyes are sad. She has dark hair and dark eyes. There's not much to her, which makes me wonder what exactly she is doing here and what they are doing to her.

"Who are you?"

"I'm Shelby," she says quietly. "I'm here to get you ready for the presentation."

That doesn't sound good.

"The presentation? What the hell is that?" I ask a little too loudly.

She looks down at the floor as if she is scared.

"I'm sorry. I shouldn't have snapped at you," I try to say calmly. She looks like she is about to bolt. I need some answers that she may be able to provide. I have no idea what she knows. "Let's start over. I'm Cassidy," I say, holding my hand out to her.

When she shakes my hand, I smile.

"I know it's not your fault that I'm in this position," I say, trying to make amends.

She looks up at me and I can see her eyes are a little glossy as if she is trying not to cry.

"It's ok. I would feel the same way if I were you. I hate that I have to do this to you, but if I don't, they will kill me," she says.

"Why are you even here? How did you get here?" I ask.

"They found me a few months ago. I was on my own after my parents were killed in a raid. They told me they would take care of me, and promised me a good life. What I didn't realize, is that they were just bringing me here to eventually be a breeder. I'm too young, thankfully, for them to do anything now. But they will eventually put me through everything that you are going through. Test me to see if I am a viable option for their program," she says in the worst imaginable explanation.

It makes me sick. The entire thing. I mean I know that we have to save the human race and all that but to put women through this testing and degradation, it's just disgusting.

"What is the presentation, or do I even want to know?" I ask.

She sighs.

"I am supposed to make you look nice. You will be presented to the potential male breeders. Then the males that decide they want a chance to... be with you, will be taken to the battle room to fight for you." I drop to my knees, but she continues. "After the winner is determined, you will be sent to the winner's cell with him to...," she pauses. "Well, you can fill in the rest. They give you two weeks. If nothing happens, or you don't get pregnant, you will be put back into the breeding pool where another male will get the chance to win you."

"Oh my God," is all I can manage to get out.

This sounds so brutal, so sadistic. How can they expect me to just be ok with this, how is any of this fair? I never would have imagined any of this happening. I thought my life would be completely different. I was supposed to be starting another semester of graduate school in the fall. I was supposed to be on the path to becoming a therapist. I had always wanted to work with children. I was going to help kids. But that is all just a dream now. Whatever this is, whatever this silent killer of women is, changed everything. The world is different. Everyone is afraid, and fear can make people do terrible things. Like, making men fight for the right to be with a woman. Like making that woman present herself, as if she is a prize to be won.

I feel a set of hands fall onto my shoulders. I look back and see Shelby smile sadly at me and I realize something. I have to be strong. I have to do this, for her. If I don't, they will kill her. Austin trained me to be strong. I owe it to him to do this. He would want me to stand tall, be brave, and look for any way out of this. Sitting here crying and feeling sorry for myself is not going to fix anything.

I stand up and look at Shelby and see her crying. I pull her into a hug.

"OK," I say.

"I'm so sorry, Cassidy," she says, crying.

I pull her into a hug. I know we just met, but I feel a need to protect this young girl. I know what I have been through, but I am older, and more experienced. She's just a kid. "Hey, hey, kid. Don't cry for me. I'm a tough cookie. I won't let them break me," I say, trying to reassure her.

She looks up and me, blinking away the tears, and eventually smiles.

Once she is settled, she takes me to a different room and shows me the showers. Being that I haven't had a real shower in months, I can't really complain about this part. There are a lot of soaps and things for me to choose from. I spend a good amount of time there. I wash my hair and my body. I shave my legs, which is the best feeling being that I have been walking around feeling like a sasquatch for a while now. Even though I am in hell, this feels like heaven.

By the time I am done, I feel amazing. I try not to focus on where I am going or what I have to do. Shelby helps me dry my hair and get dressed. They don't allow me much to choose from in the garment category. There are a few different slip dresses and some slip-on shoes, that's it. I guess they want as much of me on display as they can get.

When we are done, I do a little spin for Shelby.

"Well, what do you think?" I ask her.

"You look beautiful," she says sadly.

"Hey, now. I told you, I'm fine. I can take care of myself."

"You don't know the type of men that they have here. You won't be able to," she cries.

"You don't know me very well, but I am not a sit-and-just-take-it kind of girl. I will find a way out of here. And when I do, I'll get help and come back for you. I promise," I say, trying to assure her.

I walk over to her and wrap her in my arms.

"Listen to me, Shelby. I know it seems impossible, but I will find a way. My brother Austin was a Marine, and he taught me everything he knows. And I'm feisty, too. So, if there is any way, I will find it. I won't forget about you," I say.

"You would really come back for me?" she asks hopefully.

"Of course, I would, kid. You are kind of growing on me. Besides, what kind of person would I be if I left you here to go through the same thing?"

We end up sitting on the floor talking for a while. She tells me about growing up in New York City. Her parents survived the original hit and they headed south, to where her aunt and uncle lived in Charlotte. They got caught up in a riot and her parents died protecting her. She was on her own for a while before they caught her and brought her in. She was in high school, a sophomore. She wanted to be a veterinarian when she grew up. But like the rest of us, our hopes and dreams have changed. Now, the only thing she wants is to get out of here and not be used.

After a while, the door opens, and Mister Grumpy comes in.

"Let's go, girl," he says in his growly voice.

"Hey! Watch your tone with her. She's just a kid," I say in a warning.

"You are really in no position to give orders, Miss Daniels," he says. "I would watch *your* tone."

I sneer at him and walk over to Shelby. I pull her into a hug.

"Keep your head up, kid. Things are never as bad as they seem. The future is yet to be written. You never know what will happen," I say.

"Awe. Such inspiring words from a woman who is about to be imprisoned," Mister Grumpy says, taunting me.

I ignore him and turn back to Shelby. I palm her cheek and wink at her.

"I will see you again," I say in a whisper.

She nods, then turns and leaves with Mister Grumpy, and I'm left alone.

It feels like hours that I just sit there and wait. I look around the room, trying to find anything that I can use as a weapon or an escape. But all I see is white. White walls, white floors, white ceiling. No furniture, nothing to sit on. No windows. The door is solid steel with no handle on the inside – it is even painted, you guessed it, white. There's not even a light switch.

I look closer at what I was told to dress in. It is a simple white maxi dress that comes to my knees. Of course, they didn't give me underwear or a bra, so I am a little scared that this might be see-through. I have no idea what I am going to be walking into. What little bit of information Shelby told me scared the crap out of me.

I am to be presented to the viable men. Viable. I am really starting to hate that word.

Then, these men are going to fight for me. Why are they making them fight for me? It makes no sense.

But... then what?

That's the part that scares me. Oh, I know exactly what they expect to happen. It's the how that frightens me. Will I be forced?

I sit down on the floor, probably because there isn't anywhere else to sit and wait.

And wait.

And wait.

3

The Presentation

Mister Grumpy comes into the room with his clipboard and a couple of, what I would call, thugs. They look like bags of meat; their shirts and pants are lumpy with muscles coming from everywhere. They are both wearing clothing that is way too tight, to show off their physiques, I presume. One has dark hair and dark eyes with a scar running down the left side of his face. The other, blonde with blue eyes, looks like he could be a stunt double for Brad Pitt, but with a lot more bulk.

"Let's go, Miss Daniels. Your fate awaits."

I don't move. I don't even acknowledge him.

"Would you like me to get more of the... incentive for you, Miss Daniels?"

I really don't want any more of his magic elixir, but I really enjoy pissing him off. So, I don't move.

I am not expecting what comes next.

He backhands me across the face and then kicks me in the ribs. Hard. I do my best not to show any emotion, but I'm not the soldier. That's my brother. So instead, I let out a loud grunt, and wrap my arms around myself, falling to the floor.

"Now. Are we ready, Miss Daniels?" he asks with a sadistic smile.

"You know, karma is a bitch, asshole," I hiss.

"My name is Dr. Anderson. You can address me as such."

"I like Mister Grumpy or asshole much better," I say with a laugh, but then double over. Yup. He definitely bruised some ribs, I'm sure.

"Now! Miss Daniels," he says, barking his order loudly.

The two goons with him come over and pick me up off the ground. I groan from the pain but stand and shove their hands off me.

"Get your gropy hands off of me!" They chuckle.

"This one's got some spirit, boss," one of the goons says.

Once I am standing, they come back over to me, and each grabs an arm. They drag me out the door and down a long hallway. I'm immediately focused, checking out my surroundings and everyone that we pass. There are a lot of these goon-type guys roaming around. But absolutely no women, of any age.

Every man that I see is armed, wearing all black. I would say swat team, but what do I know? They are all ready for action, that much I can tell. I still can't tell what type of facility this is, but it is not pleasant in any way.

I'm quiet as we make our way down the hall. There are doors everywhere, but nothing that indicates where I am. Everything is plain. The floors and walls are bare. Ugly, brown tiling on the floor, yellow walls. What I wouldn't give for a weapon right now.

We finally reach a door at the end of the hall, and they stop. My nerves kick in and I am suddenly very nervous.

Mister Grumpy, uh, Dr. Anderson turns to me and glares.

"You'd better behave yourself in there, Miss Daniels. These men are not as... forgiving as I am with misbehaving."

"That supposed to make me feel better?" I mumble.

"I'm not here to comfort you, dear. I'm here to make sure that you are healthy and can produce children that will survive. Now, get in there, and behave." He opens the door, and the two goons give me a shove.

I stumble into the room awkwardly. The first thing I notice is that it is extremely bright. It takes a few seconds for my eyes to adjust but when they do, I realize that it is bright because they have a spotlight shining on me.

"Over here," a gruff voice says.

I follow the sound of the voice and see an older man, dressed in what looks like sweatpants and a dirty t-shirt. He is holding a microphone. He has white hair and is missing a few teeth. I don't get any type of comfort vibe from him, which concerns me.

"Hello dear. My name is Mick, at least that's what the boys call me. I'll be walking you through your presentation here in a minute."

I go over to where he is, and he motions for me to walk forward onto a balcony of sorts. I can now see that we are on the second floor of this facility. There is a railing preventing us from falling over the edge.

I debate for a second not doing what he says. But then I remember what the grump said. *They are not at forgiving as I am.* If he considers what he did to me as anything other than cruel and unusual punishment, he is sorely mistaken. And if these men are worse, I really don't want to find out what they would do to me for not listening. Especially because there are a lot more of them, and only one of me.

I walk over to Mick and step up onto the ledge. When I do, my stomach drops into my toes. Yeah, it's bad. Worse than I ever expected. I look over the edge onto the first floor and see probably about fifty men standing there staring up at me.

Talk about a nightmare. I almost feel like that dream that everyone has had at some point in their lives. You know the one where you are standing in front of a bunch of people naked? That's how I feel right now. Thank the heavens that I have this dress. But then again, with as thin as it is, I wouldn't be surprised if they could see all my goodies right now. There is murmuring and some of the men are openly grabbing themselves. They are definitely sizing me up, that's for sure.

I cross my arms over my chest and squeeze my legs together.

"All right, gentlemen," I hear Mick say over a loudspeaker.

This seems to get the attention of everyone in the room because it falls silent, and all eyes turn toward the man with the microphone.

"We have a real treat for you today, as you can see. We've gone and gotten you boys a viable breeder!"

Cheers and yells erupt amongst the men. They are high-fiving and slapping each other on the back, like they won the lottery or something. While they are distracted, I look around at all the men, trying to see what I will be up against. They range from what looks like kids, around eighteen years old, to older men, who I would guess are in their forties. I can't imagine having to go with any of these men. It turns my stomach.

Then, I see him. He stands out because he is standing in the back, leaning against the wall, not moving a single muscle. He is definitely one of them, though. He is wearing the same jjumpsuitas the rest of the guys. But there is something different about him. It looks like the other men are giving him a wide berth, no one going near him. And he is staring right at me. He is really tall, at least six and a half feet, if I had to guess. He's got blonde hair, and even from this far away, I can tell that he has blue eyes. They stand out and make him very noticeable.

But I guess the thing that makes him stand out the most, is just how huge he is. He stands at least a half foot taller than everyone else and he is stacked. He has muscles in places I didn't know you could have them. He's not one of those meatheads, who look like they spend all their time in the gym. He is just built. I don't know whether to be scared or turned on.

The cheering dies down and they all turn their attention back to me.

"This here is Cassidy Daniels. She is twenty-four years old," he says, and then pauses. "But... The best news for you, my friends. Is that she is untouched if you know what I mean," Mick chuckles, wiggling his eyebrows. And the cheering starts again.

I turn around and glare at him. How in the hell did he know that? I mean, I know that they did an exam down there, but I had no idea that is what they were checking for. I am sure that I am bright red right now.

"Have her take it off!"

"Let us see the good stuff!"

"Take it all off, baby!"

The men are shouting all kinds of things at the man with the microphone who is just standing there like this is the best time that he has ever had.

"Now, now, gentlemen. First things first. I need to give you more details first, then we will get to the good stuff," Mick says, looking right into my eyes, smirking.

Does he mean what I think he means? He is going to make me strip down in front of all these idiots!

He goes on to tell them about me, where I am from, my family's medical history. I guess they want them to know how good of a chance I have at giving them a baby. It's sick.

I keep finding myself looking at the giant of a man in the back. He never reacts, never so much as moves a muscle at anything that is said. But he is always looking at me.

"All right boys. Now comes the part you've all been waiting for."

I turn around as I feel someone come up behind me. Before I know what is happening, the man grabs my dress and rips it up over my head.

"What the hell is wrong with you?" I scream as I scramble to cover myself up, moaning from my bruised ribs. Remember when I said that this was like that dream, where you are standing in front of a room of people completely naked? Yeah, well dream come true. Or nightmare.

I try to grab at the dress, but he holds it away from me and I end up wrapping my arms around myself and groaning from the pain. I chance a glance at the behemoth in the back. He still hasn't moved, but he is scowling and looks ready to kill someone.

"Turn around and show the men what you've got to offer honey," he says as he laughs again and makes a spinning motion with his finger.

The hoots and hollers start again. I stand up and cross one arm over my breasts and my other hand moves down to try and cover the rest. The man who grabbed my dress grabs my shoulder and spins me towards the front of the balcony. When he gets me to the front, he grabs my arms and pins them behind my back, eliciting yet another howl of pain.

This is absolutely the worst moment of my life. I cannot believe that this is what my life has become. I am standing in front of who knows how many men, completely naked and exposed. Part of me wants to cry, just break down and lose it right here in front of everyone. But the other part of me, the part that my brother trained, wants to hold my head high and prove to these men that they will not break me.

I square my shoulders and stand up tall. The man holding me ends up letting go when he figures out that I am not going to hide. No, I'm not hiding. I do something much better. I hold both of my hands out in front of me and flip every single one of these assholes the bird. This, of course, earns me some booing but also some cheers. I guess some of these men don't want a strong woman while others find my defiance attractive.

So here I am, standing strong, completely naked, and flipping off a room full of men. If momma could see me now...

I glance around the room, making eye contact with as many as I can. Some are staring back at me with disgust, and some are smirking. But the giant man, simply stares again. But as I hold his stare, he does something odd. He nods his head. Just slightly. But enough for me to see. What that means, I have no idea. Maybe it's a sign of respect. Who knows?

I feel something hit my back and realize that they just threw my dress back at me. I quickly grab it and pull it on as quickly as I can without causing too much pain. I may want to prove to these men that they can't get to me but there is no reason that I need to do it naked.

"All right, all right. Settle down, boys. Man, honey, you sure do know how to get them riled up."

I flip him off, too. Just because. And he laughs.

"You know the drill. Anyone who wants to try for this pairing, step forward now."

At first, about twenty men step forward. I gulp, probably loudly. This is not good. When am I going to learn to control my emotions?

Then, the crowd parts, and the giant man stalks forward, his eyes on me the entire time. It's almost funny how the men seem to jump to get out of his way. It's almost as if they are afraid of him.

"Well, well, well. What do we have here? Is it finally happening? Is the Beast finally putting his hat in the ring? Been here for quite a while and you haven't shown as much as the blink of an eye at any of the women we've brought in. This is going to be one hell of a brawl, boys!" Mick is making it sound like this is the event of a lifetime. He's jumping up and down, barely containing his excitement.

The funny thing is, as soon as he finishes his little rant, almost all the men who had stepped forward, slink back into the crowd. Now there are only three standing. The Beast, as they called him, and two other men.

"Come on now boys. You can't tell me you are all that afraid of the Beast? That's disappointing. But we still have three, and that's enough. Going once? Going twice?" He pauses, looking around for any more volunteers. "OK. That's it. We are ready," he turns and looks at the panel of men behind him and nods.

"Let it begin."

4

The Battle

❝You all know the rules. There are no rules. Last one standing gets the girl. I don't care if you kill each other. I don't care how you do it. Just keep fighting until we call it," Mick says, explaining the rules.

The men who will not be fighting seem to know what they need to do. They all move back, forming a circle around the other three. The first man looks to be in his late thirties. He's probably around six feet tall, with dark hair and dark eyes. He's got an athletic build but looks more like a swimmer. What I don't like about him, though, is the way he stares at me. He looks like he wants to devour me, but not in a good way.

The second man is shorter. He's probably around my age. He's built though. Not like the Beast, but you can tell that he spent a lot of time at the gym before all of this. He, too, is smirking at me. He's dark. And by dark, I mean, he has this evil aura to him. I can tell just by looking at him that he is not a pleasant person, and that is saying it nicely. And I know that if he wins, I am in serious trouble.

Then there is the Beast. For some reason, I don't like thinking of him like that. I don't know anything about him, but I feel like if it came down to it, he would protect me. That's probably stupid on my part, but there is just something about him. He stands there with confidence that I have never seen before.

The first two, I'll call them Swimmer and Muscles, are jumping around, stretching their arms and legs, ramping themselves up for the fight. But the Beast, he is standing still. He is staring at me, but he looks focused. I don't get any weird vibes from him.

At least I know who I want to win. Something tells me that he wouldn't hurt me.

A slow chant starts amongst the other guys. "Battle, battle, battle," so low you can barely hear it.

"Let's see who wants this the most. Ready?" The men in the circle fall silent. It's very quiet, you could hear a mouse fart. Mick looks at the three men, making eye contact with each of them. He waits for them to each nod that they are ready. When he is finally satisfied that they are, he shouts. "Begin!"

Nothing happens at first. The three of them are just standing there staring at each other, almost daring the other to make the first move. But then, Swimmer and Muscles look at each other and nod. They make some sort of silent agreement, and all hell breaks loose.

They both charge the Beast at full speed. The Beast lowers down as if bracing for the impact.

The collision is violent. Somehow, the Beast manages to stay on his feet. But the other two are pummeling him with fists and kicks. I honestly don't know how this man is even still standing.

The Beast must see an opening because he manages to land a blow to Muscles' chin, which knocks him back a bit. But unfortunately, Swimmer sees the Beast's momentary distraction and throws several punches that hit their mark dead on. The Beast's nose is now bleeding, and his lip is split open. He staggers and drops to one knee.

Swimmer jumps on his back and throws an arm around the Beast's neck in a chokehold. Muscles has managed to get back to his feet and charges the Beast, nailing him right in the gut with his shoulder. The three of them tumble to the ground, with Beast on the bottom.

I scream. Some of the men turn to look at me strangely. I guess it's unusual for a woman to have a favorite in the battles. Well, if there is one thing that I definitely know about myself, it's that I am not a typical female.

I turn back to the fight and see the three men rolling around on the floor, fighting for the advantage.

I begin to hear murmurs of the men's names in the crowd. It seems that Swimmer is named Devon, and Muscles is named Stone. I prefer my names, but whatever.

Devon and Stone are tiring, that much I can see. I guess you can lift all the weights in the world and have the biggest muscles, but if you don't throw some cardio in there a little, you just don't have the stamina. Which makes me giggle a little to myself. I wonder what other aspects of his life he lacks stamina.

My giggling earns me a few more stares.

I hear a loud roar and look up just in time to see Beast toss Devon and Stone off him and across the room. He is panting. He looks absolutely enraged. But then he glances over at me, almost as if checking to see if I am ok. I nod at him, and he quickly turns his attention back to the fight.

I hear a loud whistle and turn to the crowd. A grimy-looking man is standing there waving at Devon.

"Yo, Devon! Catch," a man calls out, as he tosses something shiny into the air toward him.

It's a knife. How in the world did one of the guys manage to get a knife into what is essentially a prison? Unfortunately, they did say no rules, so no one makes a move to stop him.

Devon catches the knife and smiles. He turns and glares at Beast. Before he can take a step, however, Stone tackles him to the ground. They roll around for a bit, both trying to gain control of the knife. Devon swipes at Stone, who manages to roll out of the way. He jumps to his feet and charges Devon, who is still off balance from his attack.

They roll to the ground again. I glance over to Beast, who seems perfectly content to let them fight it out. I'm sure he's hoping that one of them will be knocked out so that they can't continue. Then it will be a fair one-on-one fight.

The men erupt in cheers. I turn to see what they are screaming about and gasp. Stone is standing over Devon, who is on the ground with his throat slit. Well, I guess that is that. No rules means killing is allowed? What have I gotten myself into?

Stone turns to stare at me, smiling. I don't know if he is waiting for me to congratulate him or what, but I do the first thing that comes to my mind. I flip him off. I guess I have a signature move now.

This makes him mad, I guess, because he growls, yes, he actually growls like an animal. I glance over at Beast and see him smirk. I guess he finds it funny. This makes me laugh, which only makes Stone angrier because he screams and charges Beast.

"Look out!" I shout.

He turns just in time to deflect the knife aimed at his chest. Stone stumbles past him but quickly rights himself.

For the next few minutes, Stone swipes lazily back and forth at Beast, clearly not skilled in using the knife. This also makes me chuckle. I think I would stand a better chance against the Beast with the knife. He has no clue what he is doing, and Beast almost looks bored with the fight at this point, which makes me think he is toying with him.

The men around the room are going nuts, chanting for Stone.

Then, almost as quickly as he killed Devon, Stone loses control of the knife as Beast grabs at his arm. The knife flips in the air. Time slows down as the rest seems to happen in slow motion.

Beast grabs the knife out of the air, grips it, then stabs Stone right in the heart. He drops to the ground immediately.

Stone is dead.

And Beast is the winner.

5

The Winner

❝ And the winner is... the Beast!"

Cheers erupt from the men, which makes me think that they didn't care who won, they just wanted to see some blood. Typical men.

"All right you heathens, back to your cells. Let the happy couple get acquainted," Mick says.

The room begins to empty. As it clears out, Mick makes his way over to me. He leads me down to the fighting area. Once there, I feel a presence behind me and turn to see Beast standing there. He is bleeding from several wounds on his head and face. There is bruising already forming there. I'm sure the rest of him is a mess as well. He took quite a beating when they teamed up on him.

"Here's the deal, you two. You have two weeks. Two weeks to complete this pairing. We will be watching. No funny business," he says in warning, looking directly at Beast, who just shrugs.

He turns to look at me next. "You will be staying in his cell with him. He will accompany you everywhere. My advice? Don't stray too far from him. There is nothing stopping any of the other men from trying to take you from him. As far as we are concerned, all the men here are viable breeders. We don't care who does it, as long as it's done."

"Then why do you have the battles?" I ask harshly. "Are you just sick, sadistic people who like to watch men die?"

He laughs. "Pretty much."

As he turns to leave, I begin to feel nervous about being alone with this man I know nothing about. I have convinced myself that I can trust him, but really, for all I know, he could be just like the rest of the men here.

I turn slowly and look up at him. Once we are alone, he sways a little on his feet.

"Whoa, big guy. Are you ok?" I ask, holding my hands up towards him as if I could catch him.

He shakes his head and nods once.

OK. Guess he's not much of a talker.

He turns and walks towards the door, stopping to look back at me. He motions for me to follow him. So, I do.

We make our way through the cell block - I can now see that yes, this facility is a prison. I'm assuming that means that I will literally be locked in a cell with him for the next two weeks. Wonderful.

We get to the end of the row, and he turns into the last cell. I pause, looking around, praying for some sort of last-minute epiphany as to how to escape. But nothing. So, I sigh and walk into the cell. Not even two seconds after I walk in, the door slides shut with a slam.

I turn to look at Beast. He is sitting on the edge of his bed, with his head in his hands.

"Are you ok?" I ask quietly.

He looks up at me but doesn't say anything.

I look around the small cell. The first thing I notice is there is only one bed. There is also a toilet and a small sink in the corner. And that's it. All in all, the room is about eight feet by eight feet of solid cinderblock. Not very homey.

I make my way over to the sink. There is a small mirror hanging above it. I glance at myself and see a bruise forming over my left cheek, where the asshole backhanded me. I run my fingers across the bruise and hear a growl. I turn to see him staring at me. I think he is growling at the bruise.

"It's nothing," I say and turn back towards the sink. I find a small hand towel on the side. I wet it with some water and go over to sit next to him on the bed. He looks over at me questioningly.

"I need to clean up your wounds. I assume you don't want them to get infected," I say.

He nods. I gently clean the wounds on his face. I can feel him staring at me as I work. Surprisingly, it doesn't make me nervous.

It doesn't look like his nose is broken, just cut and bleeding. His lip is split, and he has a nice bruise forming around his left eye.

"Do you want to pull down the top of your jumpsuit so that I can check your arms and chest? You took an awful lot of kicks when they were teaming up on you."

He pauses for a moment and then nods again.

"Are you not going to talk to me at all? I mean, the least you can do is tell me your name. I refuse to call you Beast," I say, snapping at him. This not talking thing and only nodding is getting on my nerves.

He doesn't answer, just unzips the top of his suit, and pulls the top down.

Well, that shut me up. He is ripped. No, beyond ripped. Wow. Just wow. I have never seen a more beautiful man in all my life. He is built, but not in a meat-head sort of way. It is very nice. He has a partial tattoo sleeve running down his left arm. It looks tribal but has some very intricate designs running through it.

I must have been staring for a while because he clears his throat. I look up to see him smirking. I throw the hand towel at him angrily.

"Clean yourself," I say angrily, embarrassed that he caught me.

This is the point where I wish I could storm off and leave the room. But unfortunately, that is not an option. So, I storm over to the corner farthest away from him and slump to the floor. I let out a yelp of pain. Obviously, in my drooling over him, I forgot about my bruised ribs. I wrap my arms around my middle and slump against the wall. Stupid Dr. Anderson and his boot. I wish I would have gotten a few hits in myself. I would love to see him bleed.

I hear shuffling around and then feel the big guy sit down next to me. I glance up at him. His face is extremely hard to read.

"Is there something you need?" I ask.

He holds up what looks like a roll of athletic tape. I have no idea where he got it. He must have a stash of things hidden somewhere in the cell.

Is that supposed to mean something to me?"

He points to my ribs, and it hits me. He wants to wrap my ribs so that they don't hurt as much. Now I feel bad for being so short with him.

"Sure. Thanks," I say, turning to the side.

He doesn't move.

"Are you going to do this, or what?" I ask after a minute.

He motions to my dress. Shit. I will have to take it off for him to be able to tape me, which will leave me completely naked in front of him. That is so not going got happen.

"You know what, I'm fine. I don't need you to tape them."

He gets back up and goes over to the bed. He comes back with a blanket, which he lays over my lap. After that, he begins to pull my dress up, and I quickly stop him.

"Nope! No way. Not going there," I say.

He chuckles, which is the first noise I have heard him make. I turn to scowl at him.

He holds his hands up, palms facing me. After a few seconds, he reaches for the end of my dress again and slowly begins to lift it. I know that I need my ribs taped, so I just squeeze my eyes closed and let him lift it. He stops, right below my breasts ,and ties the dress into a knot at my back, holding the dress in place. Between my dress and the blanket, I am completely covered.

I blush.

"Thank you," I say quietly.

He nods and silently begins to tape up my side. When he is finished, he turns to me and raises his eyebrows, as if asking me how it feels.

I nod. "I'm good now."

He nods again and then goes back to the bed.

We sit in silence for a while, him on the bed, me on the floor. I feel the events of the past couple of days catch up to me and unfortunately start to cry. I may maintain a rough exterior, but on the inside, I feel like a fragile little girl, at least right now. All I want is my parents and my brother back. I want all of this to go away. I don't want to have to be strong. I don't want to be this thing. This breeder. I don't want to be viable. Is that what I've become? Is that all I am good for anymore?

I spent so much time on the run. After everything happened, and our parents died, it was just Austin and me for the longest time. We ran for months, hiding, surviving. He was my rock. And then he was taken from me, too. And I was on my own, running, hiding, surviving all alone. I don't even know how long I was on my own. I lost track of time. I lost track of everything. All I knew was survival. And I failed at that because look where I am now.

I feel so alone. I feel so helpless. I hate feeling like this, but I don't know what else to do right now.

It feels as if the world is ending. Some stupid virus or whatever decides to kill almost all of the women in the world, and I am stuck with the responsibility of repopulating the Earth.

Wow, dramatic much?

Maybe it is my responsibility to help with the situation. I mean, if I can have children that will survive, shouldn't I help? That's not how I imagined becoming a mother, having a family. I wanted the dream. The caring husband, the little house, a dog. I wanted love. Another dream killed.

After a while, I feel him sit down next to me and wrap his arm around my shoulder. Without even thinking, I lean into him, needing comfort right now.

"Please tell me your name," I say quietly between tears.

Nothing. Complete silence. Maybe he can't speak. Or maybe he just doesn't want to talk to me. I snuggle closer to him, enjoying his warmth. I feel so alone. But I do feel safe, which I haven't felt in a long time. For some reason, I believe this man would protect me. I just wish I knew who he was.

These thoughts are running through my mind, as I dose off on his shoulder.

6

Life in Prison

I wake up in the bed, snuggled softly under a big blanket. He must have put me here after I fell asleep. I blink my eyes and sit up. I look around the small cell and find him asleep, on the floor next to the bed. He has no blanket, no pillow. He's just sleeping on the floor.

I can't believe he gave me his bed. He doesn't even know me.

No, he doesn't know me, but he fought two other men to the death to have me. Why? I don't really think it's because he wants to, you know, have a baby with me. No. He doesn't seem the type. From the little I know about him he seems to be more of a protector. But why would he fight, why would he kill someone to protect me? It just doesn't make sense. And being that he won't even tell me his name, it doesn't seem that I will be finding out any answers any time soon. Which is so damned frustrating!

Angry from these thoughts, I nudge him with my foot.

His eyes shoot open as wide as saucers and he jumps to his feet, his eyes scanning the room for danger before they land on me. He raises his eyebrows as if asking me what's wrong.

"Listen. This not talking thing isn't working for me. I have questions for you, and I need you to answer them," I say firmly.

He shakes his head at me, dismisses me, and goes over to the toilet. Without any warning, he opens the front of his jumpsuit and starts peeing! What the...

"What are you doing?" I screech.

He shakes his head again and I growl, loudly. It's a sound of pure frustration.

"I mean... I know what you are doing but give a girl a little bit of warning next time. Geeze! Manners, dude."

He finishes going to the bathroom and turns to wash his hands.

"Listen, I need to know who you are. I need to know why you fought for me. I don't understand why you would go through that. Help me understand. Please," I say, sounding desperate.

He doesn't respond. He shows no emotion, whatsoever. He just turns away from the sink and sits down at the other end of the bed, as far away from me as he can.

"Fine! If you aren't going to talk to me, don't expect me to talk to you! I can play the silent treatment too!"

I know I'm being a brat right now, but you have no idea how frustrated I am being in this situation and not knowing anything. None of this makes any sense. None of it! Is he expecting me to just throw myself at him? Am I supposed to just lie down and let him take care of business? Because, that just doesn't work for me, at all.

I get up again and go over to the bars. I can't look at him right now. I wish I had a different room I could go in, but I'm stuck. Stuck here in this small room with a man who saved me but won't talk to me.

I'm not sure how much time passes. I am sitting on the floor now. There is nothing to do here but think. I wish I had my bag with my things. I would love my journal. It always made me feel better to sit and write in it. There are so many things in that journal. I would write my favorite quotes, some passages from books and songs that I love, and my dreams. It is my life, all wrapped up in a little book.

At some point, they bring us lunch. I call it lunch, but really it is just some bread and what looks like oatmeal, or potatoes, or gruel. I'm not really sure what it is. I have lost my appetite, so I just push it away. The big guy grabs his and goes to town.

After lunch, he spent his time working out. He did push-ups and crunches, pull-ups on the bars of the door, and what looks like boxing. He is drenched in sweat and looking so damn good, I am finding it hard not to just sit here and enjoy the show. But I don't want to give him that satisfaction. He already smirked at me when he caught me checking him out after he lowered his jumpsuit.

I gave in and tried to talk to him a few times throughout the day, but all he does is ignore me. He doesn't even acknowledge that he heard me. Maybe that's it. Maybe he's deaf and therefore can't hear me or speak.

With this new revelation, I decided to test him out.

I wait until he has his back to me, doing more pushups, and I say something.

"You know, sitting here watching you do all of these pushups is really turning me on," I say quietly.

He immediately stops but doesn't look at me. Uh oh.

After a few heated seconds, he goes back to his workout.

Hmm. Maybe it was just a fluke, and he didn't hear me.

Test number two.

"I mean, if this is going to be how we spend our time together, I'm going to end up touching myself."

He falls to the ground. Oh shit.

He gets up and storms over to the door of the cell without looking at me. He bangs the bars a few times with his fist. Still, not looking at me. After a minute, a guard shows up. He whispers something to the guard, who immediately opens the door, and escorts him out. The guard glances back at me smirking, before leading him away. He never once looks at me.

Great, just great. Not only can he hear, but he can speak. He said something to the guard. I didn't hear what it was, but he spoke. So why won't he speak to me?

A little while later, the same guard comes back and opens the door.

"Shower time little lady," he says.

"What do you mean, shower time?" I ask, afraid he is leading me into something else.

"You see, there are these things called showers, where you can wash your hair and bathe yourself. People have been using them for a while now. Would've thought you'd heard of them before."

"Smart ass. What I meant is, how do I know you aren't taking me somewhere else? Somewhere I would get hurt, or worse," I say dryly.

"Beast just finished with his shower, and he asked me to bring you down for yours. That way he can make sure you aren't messed with in there. It's not exactly... safe for you to be anywhere on your own right now," he says. Sounds legit.

"Can I trust you?"

He laughs.

"Honey, I am about the only one in here, besides Beast that is, that you can trust," he says.

"What is your name?" I ask him. "I mean, if I can supposedly trust you, I should at least know your name."

"Jaxson. But everyone here calls me Jax."

"I'm Cassidy," I say, holding my hand out to him to shake. He takes my hand, smiling.

"Can you tell me what his name is? The Beast, I mean," I ask, hoping to get some sort of information on him.

"Afraid not, sweetheart. He's a pretty private guy, doesn't really speak to anyone in here besides me," Jax says.

"And why is that? Why won't he speak to me? I mean, he killed a guy to "win" me," I say, making air quotes with my fingers.

"That's his business, kid. I can't explain him any more than you can."

"So, I'm just supposed to spend the next couple of weeks locked up with a man who won't even tell me his name," I growl.

He chuckles. "You sure do have some spirit, Cassidy. He's going to have his hands full with you."

I make my way out of the cell and follow Jax to the showers. The entire walk there, men are leering at me from their cells. They call me names and say vulgar things making me feel dirty. One guy tells me he will see me real soon. What the hell does that mean?

We get to the showers safely. My heart drops when I see it is an open room with shower heads all along the walls. No private showers.

The big guy, because I refuse to call him Beast, is standing along the one wall, holding what looks like a towel and some clothes.

"I sure hope you aren't expecting me to shower in this big empty room. There is no way in hell I am getting naked in front of you two," I say harshly.

"Well, for starters, both of us have already seen you naked, thanks to your presentation. Yeah, I was in the room too, sweetheart," Jax says, which earns a growl from the big guy.

When I start to complain, he continues. "And secondly, I am leaving you here. Beast will protect you."

I look over to the big guy, who just nods once as if agreeing with Jax.

"Well, I'll leave you to it. Let me know when you're done Beast," Jax says, then turns and leaves us alone.

Before I can say anything, the big guy unfolds what looks to be a sheet, and holds it up in front of him, blocking his face and anyone else from seeing me. The way he is holding the sheet creates a small shower stall for me. He is giving me privacy.

"Thank you," I say quietly.

I turn around and notice that there are a few bottles sitting on a shelf. There is shampoo, conditioner, and body wash. I smile, knowing somehow that he had something to do with this being here. I'm sure that they are probably not normally things offered to the prisoners.

I quickly wash my hair and body, only lingering under the warm water for a few extra minutes.

I clear my throat.

"Um... I'm done," I say, not knowing what I am supposed to do next.

He begins to drop the sheet, so I immediately try to cover myself. But to my surprise, he has his head turned to the side and his eyes closed. He hands me a towel. After I quickly dry off and clear my throat again, he hands me some clothes. I am grateful that it is a pair of cotton pants and a long sleeve shirt. Still no underwear or bra, but at least it is more than a sheer dress. I notice a pair of slip-on shoes sitting on the floor and grab them, putting them on.

"I'm done. Thank you," I say.

He turns his head back and opens his eyes. I see him run his eyes, up and down my body. He stops and stares at me for a moment. I begin to feel a tightness in my middle. I would love to know what he is thinking right now.

He seems to realize that he is staring, so he shakes his head, and nods for me to follow him.

We walk to the door to the room, and he knocks on it. Within seconds, it opens, and Jax is standing there smiling.

"That was quick," he says. "Come on, then. Back to your cell you two."

We follow him out of the room. The big guy hangs back and motions for me to go in front of him. I hesitate, not sure if I would rather him be behind me or in front of me for protection. I don't really have a good feel for this place and with the way they made it sound, people may try and take me from him.

I guess I hesitate a little too long because Jax stops and turns around. "He wants you between the two of us because that way you are protected from both sides," he says in explanation.

The big guy nods and guides me in front of him with his hand on the small of my back. It's an intimate gesture that gives me goosebumps. I'm finding myself more and more attracted to this mysterious man the more time that I spend with him. It's the little things that he does that are getting to me.

We make our way back to the cell. With the big guy behind me, there are fewer catcalls and staring. These men are definitely scared of him. The only one who dares to say anything is the one who told me he would see me soon. He calls me sweetheart and says he can't wait to have me. The big guy stops and glares at him. The man backs away and laughs, knowing he got to him.

I scoot past him and hurry to catch up to Jax, who seems oblivious to the interaction. We make it back to our cell and Jax leaves us telling us that dinner will be up shortly.

Great. More time alone with him. I know how I want to spend the time.

"So, big guy. Do you want to explain to me why you can talk to Jax but not to me?"

7

Planning

" Are you kidding me right now?" I scream at him.

He is laying on the bed with his hands behind his head. And he is again, ignoring me. No acknowledgment that I am speaking, no answers, nothing. He is the most infuriating man on the planet! And I intend to make him aware of this fact.

"Did you go to college? I was just wondering because it seems as though you did, and your major was how to piss off a woman! There is absolutely no reason you can't answer me. I mean really. You won't even tell me your name, for God's sake. That is absolutely absurd! We are supposed to spend the next two weeks together. We are supposed to... make a baby together! What is wrong with you?" I yell as loud as I can.

This earns me a sideward glance, which just pisses me off even more.

"I don't understand any of this, at all," I say, losing my fire. "First, I lose my mom to this horrible thing, whatever it is. Then, my dad is killed trying to protect me. I spend months on the run, hiding from everyone with my brother. My brother, who by the way, is then shot and probably also killed trying to protect me. Do you have any idea how it feels to lose your whole family? Do you? I've lost everything! And then, on top of all of that, I end up abducted by a bunch of crazy people, who lock me in a cell with a man who murdered to get me here, only to have him not want anything to do with me! If I'm not mistaken, if we don't do what we are supposed to do, sometime in the next two weeks, I will be put back on the chopping block, so to speak. And even though you won't speak to me or even acknowledge my existence, you are protecting me, so I can't really complain. But, if I end up back out there, I could end up with some psycho! I am tired of running. I am tired of being afraid, every second of my life. I want my family back. I want my brother to hold me and tell me everything is going to be ok like he always did when I was freaking out. I want to know where he is and if he's ok. Because in my heart, I think he is still out there somewhere. And that tears me apart even more. He was shot! Is he out there slowly bleeding to death, or worse, dying of an infection that is so painful he is in agony? As much as it pains me to say it, if that's the case, I would wish he was dead. Because I would hate that he is going through that all because he was trying to protect me. I am already responsible for getting my father killed. I don't think I could take it if I knew I was also responsible for getting Austin killed."

Austin. I can't even think of his name without tearing up. I feel the tears running down my cheek, but I just can't keep it in anymore.

"I want my things. My bag that I had with me. I need my journal. I need the pictures of my family. I need..." I trail off, not wanting to continue anymore.

I slump down to the floor. I just don't have the strength right now. I am emotionally and physically exhausted. Last night was the first night in I don't know how long that I actually got some sleep. When you are on the run, you tend to sleep with one eye open, so to speak. I would startle at the slightest sound, which doesn't allow for that deep sleep that we all need.

I have been so worried about Austin, that I haven't really been able to even fall asleep. Every time I closed my eyes, I would picture him, laying somewhere dying. Every time I closed my eyes.

None of this is ok.

I am not ok.

· · · ·

They bring dinner to us a bit later. Dinner, which consists of the same slop from lunch, more bread, and this time, a piece of what looks like meat. But I'm not quite sure what it is. I shove it back and turn away.

The tray is slid back at me. The big guy is sitting on the floor in front of me. He raises his eyebrows, again, asking a silent question.

"I'm not a mind reader. If you want me to understand what you want, you're going to have to speak to me," I say.

He holds the tray up to me again.

"You want me to eat?"

He nods.

"I'm not hungry. You eat it," I say.

He shakes his head and shoves the tray at me again. But this time, he grabs my hand and makes me take the tray.

"Fine! I will eat if you leave me alone!"

He nods again.

I begin to eat some of the slop on the tray. It turns out it is mashed potatoes. And it's really not bad. I eat all of that and the bread. I'm afraid to try the slab of mystery meat. I hear the big guy clear his throat. As I look over at him, he makes it a point to show me his meat before he takes a bite. He seems to enjoy it, so I take a small bite of mine. It's a hamburger patty, just doesn't look like one.

After I finish my meal, he takes my tray and goes back over to the bed.

"Thank you. I needed that," I say.

He just lays down in the same position he was in before.

After a while, I feel the big guy scoop me up and lay me on the bed. I must have dozed off at some point. He places me down and I immediately roll over and curl up into a ball. He lays a blanket over me. I hear him lie down on the floor next to the bed. I immediately feel guilty that he is again giving me the bed while he lays on the cold hard floor.

I sit up, grab the blanket and pillow, and lay them on the floor next to him. He tries to give them back to me, but I refuse.

"If you want me to sleep in the bed while you are on the floor, you need to take the blanket and pillow. That's the deal. It's the least I can do," I say.

He looks angry.

"Listen. I must warn you that I am one of the most stubborn people on the planet. There is no way you are going to win this argument. The only way I am taking the blanket and pillow is if you take the bed and I take the floor. It's your choice," I say, watching his scowl.

He shakes his head at me, grabs the blanket and pillow, and turns to lie on his side facing away from me. I can't be sure, but I swear I hear him whisper "damn stubborn woman."

I smile, as I roll over and fall asleep.

I wake up the next morning with the blanket over me and the pillow next to my head. I chuckle a little, knowing that he probably just waited until I fell asleep and put them back on the bed.

And for that, I like him just a little bit more.

I hear whispering and look around. I see the big guy, standing at the cell door, talking quietly with Jax. I can't make out much, but I hear things like "will be ready in time" and "doing everything I can." I have no idea what they mean.

I sit up, which draws their attention.

"Well, boys. What are we talking about today?" I ask, and Jax laughs.

"I don't know, Beast. This one is quite lively. Are you sure she's worth it?" Jax asks, teasing him.

"Worth what? What are you talking about?"

The big guy shoots him a look, which makes him quiet.

"Well, on that note, I'll talk to you later, Beast. Behave you two," he says as he turns to leave.

The big guy shakes his head and rubs between his eyes as if he has a headache. Once Jax walks away, he comes to the toilet and looks at me.

"What was that all about?" I ask.

He just shakes his head at me and jerks his head up, as if telling me to turn around.

"I'm sorry. But the little head jerks and nods are getting old. Why don't you just tell me what you want?" I say to him.

I know he wants me to turn around so that he can use the toilet, but I am in the mood to mess with him a little.

He sighs and looks at me with his eyebrows raised and points to the toilet.

"That is called a toilet. Say it with me, toy-let," I say, being a smartass.

He growls, which makes me laugh.

"Ok. So, we have graduated from nods and points to growling. Maybe in another day, you will start grunting," I say.

He glares at me for a few seconds and then shrugs. The next thing I know, he whips it out and begins to pee. I quickly turn away and hear him chuckling.

"Jackass."

He knows he has the upper hand here and he is using it to the best of his abilities. When he is finished, he heads back over to the bed and lays down. I need to use the toilet too, so I get up and make my way over. Before I drop my pants, I stare at him for a few seconds. He hasn't as much as peeked at me yet, but that doesn't mean that I have to trust him.

"I have to pee so don't look," I say to him.

I see his shoulders shaking as if he is laughing.

I sit down and do my business quickly, not wanting to chance him looking or someone else walking by. I wash my hands and head back over to sit on the floor. It's only been a day and a half, and I am already bored.

The next few days pass in the same manner. We get up in the morning. He works out while I watch. We eat lunch. Then shower in the afternoon. He works out again. Then dinner. After an exciting evening of nothing, we go to bed.

I begin to work out with him on the fifth day, my ribs are feeling better so why not. I figure it can't hurt to keep in shape. You never know when an opportunity to run might come up. He seems pleased that I want to work out with him, so he helps me. He shows me different exercises that I can do. He tries to explain, without talking, what muscles I am working by pointing. I can't say that I love working out, but it does kill time. The days don't seem quite as long.

8

Follow Up

After the first week, something unexpected happens. We are in the middle of working out one afternoon when Jax comes up carrying a box.

"Well, good afternoon to my favorite couple," he says.

This earns a scowl from both of us.

Jax looks at the big guy and nods, which causes him to rush over to the bars. They have a quiet conversation again. I have long since given up on trying to hear what they are talking about. They have somehow mastered the art of communicating with only the barest of whispers and some kind of coded language. The little bit that I have heard, makes absolutely no sense to me. They talk at some point each day. About what, I have no idea. But if I had to guess, it's almost as if they are planning something.

Jax opens the door and hands the box to the big guy. He quickly closes the door.

"Dinner is in an hour you two. Do try to be decent when it is delivered," he says, laughing as he walks away.

When we are alone, he turns to me and smiles.

"What is it, Lassie? Did Timmy fall down the well again?"

He actually chuckles. He makes his way over to where I am sitting on the bed. He places the box down next to me and sits on the other side.

"What?" I ask.

He pushes the box closer to me and raises his eyebrows.

"Awe. Did you get me a present? What is it, our one-week anniversary? And here I thought that one week was roses, not boxes."

He frowns and shakes his head.

"Sorry. I guess I should have listed that I am a major smart ass in my personal ad," I say.

He lifts the lid off the box, and I gasp. It is my bag. The one that I was carrying when they took me.

"My bag," I say quietly. "How in the world did you get this?"

I slowly reach in and take it out. I unzip the bag and start pulling out my belongings. It's all here. My journal, my pictures of my family, and some clothes. But the most important thing is my teddy bear. It's not a large bear, only about eight inches tall. It's brown, wearing a camouflage shirt that says, "My Brother is a Marine."

I hold it to my chest.

I glance over at him and see him fighting a laugh. I know exactly what he is thinking. What is a twenty-four-year-old woman doing with a teddy bear?

"My brother, Austin, gave it to me the day he left for boot camp. It was all I had left of him when he went away," I say, trying to explain my reaction.

His laughter dies and he looks away.

"I know it's silly to have a teddy bear at my age. It's just something that always makes me think of Austin. Whenever I was missing him, I would hold it and for some stupid reason, I would feel like he was with me, no matter how far away he was. I was only thirteen when he went away. I knew it was something he had always wanted to do. He knew how much I didn't want him to go. He was my rock. Don't get me wrong, my parents were great, but there was something special in our connection. I knew that no matter what happened, I could go to him, and he would take care of me. And now he is probably gone, and it's all my fault."

I break down, squeezing the life out of my bear, wishing like hell I knew that Austin was ok. After a while, I look over at him and see him leaning forward, with his elbows on his knees and his head in his hands. I have no idea what is going through his head right now.

I wipe my eyes and try to get myself under control.

I go through the rest of my bag, and everything is there. He hasn't moved so I take it as a sign that he wants to be left alone. I put everything back in my bag, except for my journal, and go over to the corner. I sit down and open my journal.

I begin to write. I write everything that happened since they found me. It's probably slightly sadistic, but I want my story written so that if something happens to me, someone can read it and see what is going on in the world right now. I write about the torture, the questioning, the testing. How I felt when I was put on display, like a prize mare in a horse auction. I write about how I am feeling something for this quiet man. How I have come to care deeply about this mysterious man that I live with yet know nothing about. How I didn't think it was possible to care so deeply for someone in such a short amount of time.

I try to include everything.

I have kept this journal since my parents got it for me on my fourteenth birthday. It's kind of fun to go back through it every now and then, especially now that the world has gone to shit. To read about my "problems" from high school. Like when Shane Miller asked me to the homecoming dance, only to leave me for Carolyn Trotter when we got there. That felt like the end of the world to me, little did I know that ten years later I would in fact experience the actual end of the world.

I also wrote about the time Austin came home on leave when I was eighteen for my high school graduation. We had a big party at the house to celebrate. After my parents went to bed, my best friend Abby and I snuck some beers and went up to my room. Austin found us a few hours later and we were completely wasted. He put us both to bed and hid all the evidence so that our parents wouldn't find out. He gave me a lecture the next day, but I will never forget how he covered for me.

I keep trying to convince myself that if he were dead, I would feel it. There is just something in me saying that he is still alive. I just have to find a way out of here so that I can find him. Maybe I can convince the big guy to help me escape.

I am in the middle of reminiscing when a shadow appears in the doorway. I look up, and my dear friend Dr. Anderson is standing there with a terrible sneer on his face.

"Awe, did you miss me?" I ask him.

He laughs, but not a laugh that suggests he is amused by my joke. "Oh, Miss Daniels, how I love your sense of humor. You are definitely one of a kind," he says with a menacing tone.

I stand up and back away from the door, not wanting to be close to him. The big guy doesn't move from the bed. I don't even know if he has noticed that we have company, or if he cares.

"What do you want, asshole?" I ask, using my nickname for him.

"I came to check your progress."

Uh oh. What does that mean?

"If you would please, come with me, Miss Daniels," he says, opening the door.

I involuntarily take a step back. I recognize his two goons from before. They come in and grab me. As I am dragged out of the cell, I look over to the big guy, who is now sitting up in the bed. He looks angry but doesn't make a move to help me. They drag me down the entire cell block. I wasn't kicking or screaming, but I certainly wasn't making it easy on them. We continue into the medical area that I was in when they brought me here.

Once I'm back in the room, yes, the torture room, they throw me on the bed and leave. Dr. Anderson comes over and secures my arms and legs. Well, this certainly seems familiar.

A man comes in, a doctor I guess because he is wearing a lab coat. He puts on a pair of gloves and drags a tray over to the table. I recognize the instruments. They are the same ones they used when they did the exam... down there, if you know what I mean.

I don't struggle. It's bad enough what they are doing, I don't want to add any further discomfort or pain to what they are doing. He pulls my pants off and begins his exam.

I have had more than enough of the way this man treats me. It's like he has a personal vendetta against me. Not two seconds after the man starts, he looks at Dr. Anderson and shakes his head. Anderson looks furious.

"This is not a vacation, Miss Daniels. You have a duty to fulfill. You have one more week and that's it. If you don't do what you must, I will choose someone who will take care of it for me. And that, my dear, will not be pleasant for you," he says, his warning clear.

I don't say a word. I can't think of anything to say that will not make this worse. So, I simply nod.

They untie me and I scramble to pull up my pants. I don't remember the trip back to the cell. The only thing I remember is being thrown back into the cell.

"Remember Miss Daniels. One more week, then you are mine," he says in a final warning and walks away.

I collapse onto the floor. The big guy is just sitting there, looking at me with a blank expression. Once Anderson walks away, he comes over and sits next to me. Normally, I would want comfort, but he did nothing to stop them from taking me. He just sat there.

"Go away," I say quietly.

He tries to wrap his arm around me, but I push him away. "I don't want to look at you right now. Just go away," I say again.

He gets up and walks away, back to the bed. He sits down and puts his head in his hands. I can't find it in me to feel bad right now. I just can't. I sit there for a while just thinking. This just keeps getting worse and worse. I am trying not to think about what he said. *In one week, you're mine.* I shiver at the thought. My future does not look very good.

I glance over at the big guy and see him in the same position. I start to feel bad. What did I really expect him to do? They would have hurt him if he would have interfered. Maybe he knew that. He did look angry. I want to believe that this mysterious man cares for me. His actions, well sometimes, suggest that he does. But he is so hot and cold. Sometimes he cares, sometimes he is indifferent. I am so confused.

This place really does suck.

• • • •

When they bring dinner, he comes over to sit with me on the floor, like we have been doing for the past few days. He still doesn't speak but it's nice to just eat with him. Makes the loneliness go away for just a bit. In my mind, I have forgiven him for earlier. Life is too short to hold onto such anger, especially given the current world events.

He smiles at me. It is a small smile. I kind of feel like it is an apology. His smile fades and he looks upset. I pat his knee.

"It's ok. I know there isn't anything you could have done," I say. He nods, then looks down at his feet.

We sit and eat in silence. When we finish, he nods toward my journal.

"Yeah. It's my journal. I have written in it quite a bit since my parents gave it to me. It's not a "Dear Diary" sort of journal. I write my favorite quotes and song lyrics in it. I write about things that have happened to me over the years. My dreams. Well, what used to be my dreams. Not really any point to having dreams anymore, is there."

He points to it and raises his eyebrows.

"You want to read something?" I ask him. He nods.

I think about it for a second. I guess it can't hurt to let him read the story of when Abby and I got drunk at my graduation party.

"Ok," I say, turning to the right page and handing it to him. I watch his facial expressions as he reads it. I can tell when he is at certain parts by how he reacts. By the end, he is laughing out loud.

I have a new favorite sound.

"You have a really nice laugh," I say, blushing and then looking down so that he doesn't see it. I feel his finger under my chin, lifting my face up so that he can see me. We look into each other's eyes. I feel like he can see my soul right now. I feel vulnerable.

I clear my throat and take my journal back from him.

"So, now you know that I was a troublemaker growing up. I guess I need to apologize to Austin if I ever...," I trail off, not being able to finish that thought.

He lifts my hand into his and squeezes. I look into his eyes and see that they are wet, with unshed tears. He brings his other hand up and taps his chest, right over his heart.

"You can feel it in your heart that I will see him again?" I ask him.

He nods. He then brings my hand up and lays it right over his heart. I can feel his heart beating quickly. He places his other hand on my cheek and wipes away the stray tears that have fallen.

And just like that, I have fallen in love with this silent man. I don't know what it is about him. You would think the hot and cold thing would annoy me, and it has. But I guess it is just the way he cares for me when we are alone that gets to me.

It's then that I realize that the only times he is caring are when we are alone, or with Jax. When other people from the prison are around, he is indifferent. I wonder if he is trying to protect me by not letting on to them that he cares for me. If they knew, they would hurt me to get to him. Or maybe I am just crazy.

I look up at him, ready to lay it on the line, so to speak. "I know that for some reason, you don't want to talk to me. I can't say I understand it, but I respect you enough not to push you on it." I scoot closer to him so that I can whisper. After the events of today, I have no idea if they are listening to us somehow. "I want you to know that I have come to care for you. I can't explain it, but I feel safe with you. I feel like no matter what, you have my back."

He nods.

"So, I feel that I need to let you know, should the opportunity arise for me to escape, I have to take it," I say, but he shakes his head aggressively.

"No, listen. Please. You have to understand. I have to. I can't stay here and let them torture me. I know that you won't, but eventually, someone will end up raping me. And I can't let that happen. I know that you will protect me as long as I am with you, but after that, I'm on my own. You won't always be here. If we don't... If you... If I don't get pregnant, things are going to get so much worse for me. And I am not saying that I want you to knock me up. I'm just saying I am not naïve. I know what is going to happen. I lucked out with you. You are probably one of the last decent men left on the planet. And I don't want to leave you. But if I get the chance, I have to," I say, trying to explain to him what I am feeling.

He shakes his head again, looking angry now.

"Please, try to understand. Look at it from my perspective. You can't always protect me," I say, tears running down my face.

He nods this time, grabbing my hand and putting it on his chest over his heart again.

"I'm sorry, but I have to try to get out of here."

He shakes his head again and abruptly stands.

"Uh, oh. Are the lovers having a quarrel?" a disgusting, chubby man says from outside our cell. It's the man that said he would see me later. He is surrounded by five men. All of them look dirty and downright nasty. I quickly wipe the tears away from my face and stand up.

"Mind your own business, asswipe," I say angrily as I move away from the bars.

"Hey, Beast. You'd better control your woman or I'm going to have to teach her a lesson next time I find her alone," the grimy man says.

The big guy just waves his hand at the group, almost dismissing them.

Seriously, is he not going to protect me? Here we go again.

"Hey, pig! He doesn't control me. And I am not his woman! So why don't you find your way back to the pig pen before I teach you some manners," I threaten, not sure how I would do that if it came down to it.

"Oh, oh, oh. The little woman is feisty. Well, how's about I find my guard friend to come and open this door so you can teach me some manners?" he asks.

Oh, shit. When am I going to learn to keep my mouth shut?

"Go ahead, dirtball. I'm ready to kick some ass," I say, trying to sound confident.

I look back to see where the big guy is, only to find him taking a leak.

"You're lucky this door is separating us right now, sweetheart. One of these days, I'm going to fill that smart mouth of yours with something. And let me just tell you, I will certainly enjoy that day," he threatens as he and his group walk away.

I wait a minute, making sure that they are out of range before I run at the big guy.

"What the hell is wrong with you?" I ask angrily, shoving him in the back. He looks down at me and shakes his head.

"What, I tell you I need to get out of here and you won't protect me anymore?"

He waves his hand at me and goes over to lie on the bed.

"Remember when I said I cared for you, well, you can forget it. I'm done with you. As soon as I get the chance, I am out of here," I say, walking over and slumping down in the corner.

9

Out of Time

I wake in the middle of the night, again on the bed, to whispering. It sounds almost frantic. I look up to see Jax and the big guy going back and forth, the big guy looking extremely upset. This, of course, gets me interested. I lay perfectly still, trying to make it look like I am still asleep. I need to try and hear what they are saying.

"It has to happen now, Jax. We are out of time!" the big guy says.

"Things are not ready yet," Jax says.

"Well, get ready! I will not let her get hurt. I can't," he says.

They both turn to look at me and I quickly close my eyes and slow my breathing. I'm not sure if they know I am awake or not, but the conversation ends abruptly.

"Give me until tomorrow night and I'll be ready," Jax says.

They shake hands and Jax leaves.

I lay there quietly and as still as possible. He walks over to the bed, and I can feel him staring down at me. I slowly roll over so that I am facing the wall, trying to make it look natural. I even throw in a sigh for dramatic effect. I feel him pull the blanket off the floor and lay it over me. He pulls it up so that I am covered. He leans down and does something completely unexpected.

He kisses me on the forehead and whispers something in my ear. "I will always protect you." He then lays down on the floor to go to sleep.

What the hell was that? What is going on? I have a terrible feeling that something big is about to happen and I have no idea what that is. And that scares me, a lot.

· · · ·

The next morning everything seems quiet. He is going out of his way to ignore me today. I don't work out with him this time. I just sit on the bed and doodle in my journal. I am completely and utterly confused after last night. I lay awake and thought about it for a long time.

I get the feeling that he is ignoring me to protect me. Is that possible? I can't think of any other reason. But it just doesn't make sense. Why would he take care of me in other ways, like giving me the bed, and eating dinner with me, only to not talk to me? You would think that if he was doing it to protect me, he would just completely ignore me. But then again, why would he enter the fight and kill someone, just to get me here to not talk to me?

None of this makes any sense and it is really annoying the hell out of me. I am just about to get up to give him hell when Jax appears at the door.

"Shower time, you two. Let's go," he says, his usual smile absent.

It's earlier than normal for showers. We usually go after lunch, and we haven't eaten yet.

"Why so…" I start, but Jax immediately cuts me off.

"Come on, I don't have all day," he says pointedly at me, almost willing me to shut up.

I put everything back in my bag and stand up. I have been bringing my bag with me every time we leave the cell just in case I get the chance to run.

We make our way down to the showers. Something feels off, not right. I have the willies right now and I find myself looking around in all directions, waiting for the attack.

When we get down to the shower room Jax stops. He turns to the big guy.

"When you hear the alarm, make your move," he says in a whisper.

He nods and we go into the room. I notice, however, that this time, the door doesn't close the whole way.

We get inside and I make my way over to the showers, getting ready to start mine. I turn around and see that the big guy is just standing by the door.

"What are you doing?" I ask.

He looks over and me and motions with his head for me to come over to where he is. I look at him skeptically, then go over and stand next to him.

He looks down at me. He lifts his hand and caresses my cheek. I can't help it; I close my eyes and lean into him.

"No matter what happens, you need to stay behind me. Listen to everything that I tell you and we will get out of here alive," he says quietly.

I am so taken aback by hearing his voice that I jump.

"What?" is all I manage to get out.

"Cassidy, focus. Look at me," he says. "Do exactly what I tell you and stay by my side. Please."

Still in shock that he is actually talking to me, I simply nod. His voice is deep yet soothing. Not what I would have expected from such a big guy.

After a few minutes, I hear a commotion out in the hall. Shouting and cursing. At one point, a bunch of people run past the door. Guards? Prisoners? I can't tell.

Suddenly, the alarm sounds.

"Ready?" he asks, and I nod.

He grabs my hand, and we take off out the door. I look around quickly and see that there is a massive riot going on. Guards and prisoners are all over each other. I see men hitting each other with whatever they can get their hands on. Guns firing, people shouting. Chaos.

About halfway through the main room, I see Jax being pummeled by a group of men in jumpsuits. I stop, pulling him with me.

"Cassidy! We don't have time for this," he says.

"You have to help Jax! He helped us! We can't leave him here like that," I say, pointing to where Jax is being beaten.

He looks to where I am pointing and curses. "Shit!"

He looks back and forth between me and Jax. I can tell he is debating whether or not to help him or get me away. He decides quickly, because he pulls me into him, hard.

"Stay here, Cassidy. I mean it. No matter what you see or hear, do not go anywhere without me," he says.

I nod, knowing that he will come back for me.

"I swear, Cass. If you move, I will blister your sweet little ass," he says in warning.

"Just go. Jax is hurt," I say.

He kisses me on the forehead and then turns and runs to Jax. I watch as he begins grabbing men and throwing them off him. Jax is finally back on his feet and joins the big guy in the fight. The two of them together are a force to be reckoned with. They gain the upper hand quickly.

I am so engrossed in the fight, that I don't notice the group of men approaching me from my right.

"Well, well, well. Look who we have here, guys. It's sweet Cassidy with her smart mouth. If I remember right, I told her I would stick something in her mouth the next time I saw her."

It's the grimy man and his groupies from yesterday. I look around for an escape. I consider screaming but am concerned that it may draw the wrong kind of attention. I mean, Jax and the big guy can hold their own, but not against the whole place.

"You'd better leave while you can," I say in a warning.

"Oh yeah, honey? And who's going to stop me? Beast? He's otherwise engaged at the moment. So, why don't we take this somewhere more private?" he says, while his goons grab me.

They tear my bag off my back and drop it on the ground. I begin kicking and thrashing, trying to hit anything that I can. I manage to kick one of them in the nuts and hit another guy in the leg. But it's not enough to stop them. There are just too many of them and not enough of me.

They drag me down a hallway and into a cell. A couple of the guys keep watch at the door while slimeball and the rest of the guys push me over to the bed. I have never felt such all-encompassing fear before. The fear that I am about to be defiled and then killed. Something tells me these are the type of men that do not care about consequences. They just do what they want.

I am forced to my knees with my hands held behind my back. Slimeball steps up in front of me and begins to undo his jumpsuit.

"I feel the need to warn you that anything that you put in my mouth will be bitten off," I say, trying to sound tough, even though I am terrified.

"You listen to me, honey. If you do anything to hurt me, not only will my men rape you, but then they will bring lover boy in here and torture him in front of you. Then, they will kill him and then kill you. But I assure you, that each and every one of my men will have a turn with you first."

Holy shit. I am dead.

I struggle to free my arms, fighting with all my might to get free but it's no use. They are too strong.

Just before he can pull his... thing out, I hear a roar outside of the room. The two guards go flying just as a huge figure comes charging into the cell.

It doesn't take me long to recognize that it is the big guy and Jax and they are ruling the room. Slimeball tries to slip out the door while the chaos is ensuing, but he gets stopped by my savior at the last second.

"Did you think you could just take her? Did you really think I would let you hurt what's mine?" the big guy asks, but I don't think he expects an answer with the way he is seething. I have never seen him like this before.

He looks completely terrifying right now. Like he is ready to kill. Forget the fact that he just claimed me in front of all these people. He saved me.

He has Slimeball pinned to the wall by his shirt collar and is staring him down. The best thing is the wet spot slowly appearing on the front of Slimeball's pants. He made him pee himself.

The big guy turns his head and looks right at Jax.

"Get her out of here. I need a few minutes alone with him," he says to Jax. Jax simply nods. He hands me my bag and starts to pull me through the door of the cell. The rest of Slimeball's men are laying on the floor either knocked out or groaning in pain.

"Wait," I say. "I don't want to leave you."

A small smile forms on his lips – he is pleased with my request. "Don't worry. I'll be right behind you," he says to reassure me.

Jax and I make our way past the cell block and down a long hallway. At the end, there is a door that is locked.

"Don't worry. He'll be here in a minute," Jax says.

Just as he finishes his sentence, the big guy comes running down the hall. He stops right in front of me and pulls me into his arms. His hold is tight. "I'm sorry. I'm so sorry I let that happen. I promised myself I would never let anything happen to you," he says, almost to himself.

"I'm fine, really. But I need to know what is going on here," I say as I push him away. As good as it felt to be in his arms, I need answers.

"Coop. You didn't tell her," Jax asks him.

"Coop?" I ask.

I look between the two of them who seem to be having a silent conversation.

"Tell me what?" I ask, getting more annoyed.

"Come on, Jax. We don't have much time," Coop says, motioning for the door.

"No, Coop," I shout, exaggerating the P in his name. "I am tired of being in the dark. You wouldn't tell me your name. You wouldn't talk to me. Now, apparently, we are escaping, and I know nothing about it. The very least you can do is tell me what the plan is!"

Coop looks at me. I almost feel bad for him at the moment. He looks like a lost puppy. Fortunately, I focus on the fact that I am furious at him for all the secrets and am able to hold onto my anger.

"I'm sorry, Cass. There's no time. We have to get out of here now before it's too late," he tells me. He looks over at Jax and nods.

Jax goes over and quickly opens the door with his keys. He then hands Coop a couple of guns, some ammo, and a backpack.

"Do it quick and then get out of here, man," Jax says.

"Come with us," Coop says.

"Awe. Don't get sentimental on me now. Besides, you know you need someone on the inside," Jax says.

Coop nods and quickly hugs Jax.

"Thanks, man. I owe you my life," he says, right before he shoots Jax in the arm.

"Mother fucker! That hurts more than I remember," Jax curses.

I can hear the shouting and it is getting closer.

Jax looks over at me sadly.

"Take care of him, honey. Hopefully, if things go as planned, I'll see you again sometime," he says, pulling me into a quick hug.

Still completely confused as to what is happening, I just smile at him.

Coop grabs my hand and we run. And run. We get to the end of another long hallway and open the door.

Finally, we are outside.

Coop ruffles through the bag until he finds a small electronic device. He holds it up and turns it on and I see it is a compass sort of thing. He turns around back and forth for a few moments. Once he is satisfied and he decides on a direction, he grabs my hand again and we take off.

I try to talk to him, and ask questions, but he never answers. He just keeps pulling me along behind him. After a while, I give up and just follow.

We run for what feels like hours. He lets me stop for a few breaks, handing me water and granola bars. I am in decent shape, but anyone would get tired after running this much. I can't catch my breath enough to ask any more questions, and I think he is happy about that for now.

When the sun begins to set, we end up at a cave hidden in the middle of the woods somewhere. Coop pulls out a flashlight and we head inside.

What we find shocks me. There are supplies. And not just survival supplies, but weapons, equipment, food, water, blankets, and clothes. Enough to survive on for a while. I am relieved for a few seconds.

Relieved until I remember that Coop is now talking, and I still have no idea what the hell is going on.

I walk over to the pile of guns and grab the first one I see. I check the clip, put it back in, and hold it up at Coop, aiming directly at his head.

"You have about three seconds to explain what the fuck is going on before I lose my shit and start firing, Coop," I exaggerate his name now that I know it.

10

Identities and Plans Revealed

"Cass," he pleads, holding his hands up, palms forward in front of him, trying to calm me down. I guess pointing a loaded weapon at someone gets you answers quickly. Where was a gun last week when I needed it?

"Don't you Cass me! What the hell is going on? Who are you?"

He sighs and plops down in a chair by the supplies. I guess he is as tired as I am.

"My name is Cooper Matthews. I was, no am, your brother's best friend," he says calmly.

Cooper. Austin's Cooper? This shocks me, to say the least. I lower the gun.

"What... How... When did...?" I can't even finish.

"Come sit down and eat something. You must be exhausted and hungry."

"No! I need answers. How did you end up at that facility? Why couldn't you tell me who you were? Why did you ignore me and make me feel alone? Why, Cooper?" I ask the tears in my eyes threatening to fall.

He gets up and comes over to me, wrapping me in his arms. As much as I hate to admit it, it is exactly what I need right now. His body heat, his strength, his comfort.

"I'm so sorry, baby. I can't even tell you how sorry I am," he says. Baby? I push away from him.

"Whoa, whoa, whoa, Casanova. Where do you get off calling me baby?" I ask, ready to start throwing punches.

He smiles, the jerk.

"Cassidy. Please come sit and eat. I will answer all your questions, I promise. But you need to eat," he says, almost begging.

Of course, right at that moment, my stomach growls, really loudly. He smirks, again.

I concede and make my way over to the lone table and chairs. I plop into one and do not hesitate to tear off my shoes. While I am massaging my aching feet, Cooper heads back over and begins cooking something on a small camping stove. A few minutes later I begin to smell something delicious.

"Wow. I'm learning more about you in the last few hours than I have in the last week and a half that I have known you," I say sarcastically.

"Don't be too impressed. It's just a few hamburgers from the cooler that they left. And before you ask, yes, I will tell you who *they* are in a minute," he says.

He finishes our food, which consists of hamburgers, chips, and a couple of sodas. I actually moan at the taste of the soda. I haven't had one since before all of this started. I glance over at Cooper and see him staring at me, his food halfway to his mouth.

"What?"

"Please don't moan like that again if you want me to remain a gentleman," he says, which makes me blush. I didn't realize that my moan would turn him on.

He begins to eat. After a few bites, he looks over at me.

"Ask away," he says.

There are so many questions that I have but I am having a hard time deciding which ones are the most important right now. I think for a minute and finally, decide on something that has been bothering me since the beginning.

"Why wouldn't you talk to me? Why wouldn't you tell me your name?"

He sighs and puts his hamburger back on his plate. Before I know it, he is knelt in front of me, holding my hands in his. He rubs in thumbs back and forth across the back of my knuckles.

"I knew who you were the second you stepped out onto that platform. I had been in the facility for a while. I knew that you would be there at some point, I just wasn't prepared to see you so soon. Austin had been showing me your picture since we met. In a sense, I watched you grow up through those pictures. Add from all of the stories Austin used to tell me about you, I felt like I really knew you."

"But what does any of this have to do with the facility?" I ask, getting impatient.

He chuckles.

"I forgot how impatient you are. Just bear with me and I'll get there. But there are things that you need to understand before I get there."

I nod and he continues.

"As the years passed, I found myself waiting for Austin to talk about you. He did it a lot. And those were the times that I lived for, talking about you. Your eighteenth birthday is the moment that stands out in my mind the most. We were stationed in Germany at the time. Austin was chatting with you on the computer. I positioned myself across the room in the perfect place where I could see you on the screen and hear everything that you were saying, but you couldn't see me. I was completely enthralled with you at this point. But that conversation, when you were telling him all about your birthday party and upcoming graduation, I realized something. I knew right then and there that I was in love with you. You had no idea who I was, with the exception of Austin telling you about me every once in a while. But I didn't care.

"When I was in bed that night, you were all I could think about. I made a promise to myself. I vowed that I would never love another. I know it seems silly, but I could feel it. I could feel how special you are. When we got home on leave this last time, and everything happened, I remember being in an absolute panic not knowing if you had survived this... thing. I desperately tried to get ahold of Austin for days. Luckily, right before the phones crashed, he called me. He told me that you had survived, but that you and he were alone. Your parents had passed. We made plans to meet at my cabin. We knew that between the two of us, we could protect you."

I sat there completely shocked. I had no words. I had convinced myself in the facility that he wanted nothing to do with me and that was why he was ignoring me. But here, he loves me. What do you say to that? I decided to sidestep that issue for now.

"OK. We are going to table that discussion for a later date. You still haven't explained why you were ignoring me," I say.

"Getting there, love," he teases, and I roll my eyes.

"I have to explain a few other things before I can get to that, but I promise we are getting there," he says.

"Well, get there faster," I say. He chuckles.

"I belong to a group of people, mostly Marines and Army guys, that are working together to... well, to help. We grouped together back at the beginning of this... thing. When these people started abducting men and women for their facilities, we decided that someone needed to fight back. It's not that we don't believe in what they are doing, it's their methods that we disagree with. We sent some of our men to work in these facilities so that we would have men on the inside, trying to get intel on what is going on. A few months ago, I got word from one of my buddies that Austin was picked up and was in one of the facilities. Through that man, I was able to get information from Austin as to your whereabouts when he was taken. We did some recon to determine which direction you would most likely be heading and decided that if picked up, you would most likely be taken to the facility that we were at. Once we figured that out, I managed to get myself "picked up" and taken there too. I was there waiting for you, Cass. To protect you. I had a better chance of just waiting for you there than I did trying to find you on foot. There were too many variables out there to try and find you. So, that's what I did. I sat in a cell and waited."

As much as I appreciated his plan to protect me, all I am able to do is focus on the fact that I was tortured, poked and prodded, and totally and completely humiliated while he was "waiting." I pull my hands out of his hold and punch him square in the face. When he falls back, I get up and start angrily pacing back and forth in the cave.

"I tell you that I love you and that I waited for you in that facility, and you punch me? What kind of thanks is that?" he asks, rubbing his jaw.

"I was tortured! I was beaten! I was a guinea pig for their doctors. I was stripped naked and presented to a room full of men who were groping themselves while they stared at me. And then, after I survived all of that, I was shoved into a room with an idiot who wouldn't even speak to me. So, I'm sorry if I am not falling to my knees to thank you!" I scream at him.

He's silent for a moment. "They tortured and beat you?"

I nod, shivering as I remember the pain.

"What did they do?" he asks, sounding like he is in pain.

I turn away from him. I really don't want to relive this, but part of me wants to hurt him with the information. I don't want to, but I think part of me is blaming him as if it was his fault.

"He kept injecting me with these different things. Some made my entire body feel like it was on fire. Others, just pain. You name it, he had it. Even once I started to answer his questions, he kept injecting me, just because he could. It lasted hours, or maybe days. I don't even know. And then, right before my presentation, he kicked me in the ribs and backhanded me. The guy was a real asshole. Is that enough for you?"

I turn around to glare at him but stop in my tracks. He is sitting on his knees on the floor with his head down.

"I didn't know that they did that to the women. I mean we figured that they did exams and maybe took some blood, but I had never heard that they tortured and experimented on the women brought in. No one ever told me that," he says, sounding broken like I punched him in the gut.

"It doesn't matter now. It's over," I say, dismissing him, not ready to forgive him.

"It absolutely does matter," he shouts as he gets to his feet. He comes over to me and pulls me into his arms.

"I totally fucked up, Cass! I can't tell you how sorry I am. I never thought you would have to endure something like that if you got picked up. I figured that was the easiest way to find you. I should have looked for you myself, I should have just found you," he says, squeezing me.

I push away from him again and walk away. I love being in his arms. I really do. I feel so safe and loved. But after everything that he has revealed so far, I am just too angry.

"Finish your story, please," I say, sitting back down in my chair.

He just stands there for a few seconds, his hands clenched into fists at his sides. He finally makes his way back over and sits down in his chair. He seems to be having some type of battle with himself, but he eventually nods.

"Before you got there, I made it a point to stay silent. I didn't want to talk to anyone and chance letting something slip. I wanted to be known as the strong, silent guy. Within a couple of weeks, the other guys started staying away from me. I heard whispers that people thought I was insane. It helped that Jax spread some rumors about me. Anyway, when you showed up, I knew that no matter what, I had to win the battle. I figured I would have to kill some people, but I was ok with that if it meant keeping you safe. I was happy that it ended up being only two guys. And it made it even better that those guys were assholes.

"When I won, and you wanted to take care of me, I almost broke. The reason that I didn't talk to you, that I wouldn't tell you my name was because I had to protect you. If any of the other men in there knew how I felt about you, knew that I was trying to protect you, they would have gone out of their way to kill me, and then hurt you. I couldn't let that happen. No matter how much it killed me. It took everything in me not to curl up behind you on the bed every night. You have no idea how hard it was not to touch you and hold you when you were upset. I wanted to kiss you and tell you how much I love you. But I couldn't."

I look away from him. I can't hold his gaze right now, knowing that I had been wishing for those exact things.

"And don't think I forgot about your little stunt of testing my hearing when I was working out. Yeah, I knew what you were doing. I came so close to pinning you to the bed and having my way with you. You'll pay for that at some point, but not right now," he says with a devious smile.

I blush, totally forgetting that I did that.

"Anyway. From the second you stepped into that room, Jax and I were making plans for our escape. We weren't quite ready, but you pushed up the timeline when you told me that you might try to escape on your own. I knew you would get hurt without me. I'm not saying you aren't capable you just don't know everything that I know about that place. And they probably would have picked you back up sooner rather than later. And that would have been very bad for you," he says. He's right. I never thought about what would happen if I did get out. I probably would have ended up right back there with Anderson. And I know what he would do to me if he got his hands back on me.

"That last night, Jax came back to let me know that the final thing was ready. We had to wait for our people to stock this cave so that we had somewhere safe to hideout on our way to the base."

"Ok. What do you know about everything that happened? Does your group have people researching it?" I ask him.

"We know as much as anyone else. We don't have anyone in our group researching right now. None of us knew any scientists. But we have people in a lot of the facilities around this region. They are all working in different parts of the facilities. If they find out anything pertinent, they pass it on. And if they get even an inkling that someone is unhappy there, they try to get them out. So far, we have taken down four of the facilities," he explains.

"How have you taken them down? What does that mean?"

"Each one was different. Some, we caused riots, like we did today. The riots got violent enough that we were able to get a lot of people out. Enough that the facility was unable to continue. Others, we used more... forceful means," he says as he smirks.

"Why didn't we save more people today? There is a young girl, Shelby, who was with me in the hospital. We should have saved her," I shout.

"We only had one priority today," he says, trying to calm me down.

"Yeah. And what was that?" I ask angrily.

He looks at me somberly. "You," he says. "My only priority today was making sure we got you out. I didn't care what happened to me. I just wanted to make sure you were safe."

11

The Truth Hurts

After hearing everything that Cooper had to say, I excused myself. I needed some space, some time to think. I told him I was only going right outside the cave. He, of course, tried to stop me, but I told him it was either that or I was leaving. He conceded, saying that if anything happened or I saw anything, I was to come right back inside.

Outside, I find a large tree and sit down on the ground. I just sit and listen to the sounds of the forest. It is pitch black outside, probably around midnight if I had to guess. I let my mind wander, trying not to think about anything specific. I just learned so many disturbing things. As much as I hate to admit it, I keep thinking about Cooper, and everything that he went through for me.

What kind of person does that for someone they don't know? But I guess he really does kind of know me. I know how much Austin likes to talk about me. He probably knows all my most embarrassing secrets.

But the thing that gets me the most, is all the secrets. All he had to do was explain to me what was going on and I could have played along. There was no need to keep me in the dark. I suffered. Ok, maybe suffered is too strong a word. But I was definitely miserable.

I find myself laughing at this. Not because I think I am being dramatic, because I am not! And if you think that, I have a few choice words for you. No, I am thinking about Austin and the time that I gave him the silent treatment after he told me he was enlisting.

"You can't stay mad at me forever, you know," Austin said.

I was sitting in my room, curled up under the blanket on my bed. He just finished telling me how he is leaving in a few weeks for boot camp. He had enlisted. He wanted to be a Marine. He and I had talked about it through the years. I knew that is what he wanted. But I guess I never thought he would really do it.

"Go away, Aus. I am never talking to you again," I said.

Being a teenager was tough enough. My best friend was leaving me to do it alone. He was the one who was there for me when I got my period. My mom wanted to help, but I only wanted Austin. He was the one who took me out for ice cream sundaes after my first boyfriend, Brian, broke up with me. He was the one that I turned to for everything. We were five years apart in age, but he took me everywhere with him. His friends used to complain about me always being around, but he didn't care. He took care of me. Always. How was I going to survive without him?

"You know why I am doing this. We have talked about it so many times. I promise that I will write every single day and call as much as I can. Stop being dramatic," he said.

If you know anything about girls at all, it's to never tell them they are being dramatic. That's a given.

"Dramatic! I'll give you dramatic," I said as I began to throw every single one of my stuffed animals at his head. "You are leaving me! Do you know how that makes me feel? Do you really even love me? Because if you did, you wouldn't do this," I cried. It pained me to say such hurtful things to him, but I was hurting. "So just go, leave me alone. I don't want to look at you right now."

"Cass," he said. He looked completely broken.

"Just go, Austin," I cried as I dropped back onto my bed and pulled my blanket over my head.

"Ok, kid. I'll go. But this isn't over," he said sadly.

He left my room, closing the door quietly behind him. When I heard the click of the door, I completely lost it. I lay in my bed and cried for hours. You would think I would have passed out at some point but not me. I was as stubborn as a mule. I sat there for hours convincing myself that I hated him. He wanted to leave me. How could he?

After a while, I started to really think. All I could think about is that he would leave, and something would happen to him. And that's when it hit me.

I was terrified that I was going to lose him. You heard all the time about soldiers who were killed in action, about things happening and people dying. I couldn't imagine losing him. He may have been going away, but he was still my brother and best friend. I couldn't let him leave thinking that I hated him.

So, I jumped out of bed and went tearing through the house trying to find him.

"Austin, Austin, Austin!"

"What, Cass," he said, stepping out of the kitchen where he had been talking with my parents.

I turned the corner and jumped into his arms.

"I don't want to lose you," I cried.

"Awe, kid. You're not going to lose me, I promise. I'm just as stubborn as you are, remember? I won't ever let anything happen so that I can't make it home to you. I love you more than anything. You're my best friend," he said soothingly.

I feel the tears running down my face and wipe them away. I miss my brother. After a while, I hear Cooper come out of the cave. He makes his way over to me and plops down. He nudges my shoulder.

"So, on a scale of one to ten, how much do you hate me right now?" he asks me.

"I'm hovering in the low to mid-forties," I say, nudging him back.

"Cass, I never meant to hurt you. That is the last thing that I would ever want to do," he says quietly.

I can tell he means it. He has his hands in his lap and he is playing with his fingers. I want to forgive him, I really do. But the whole silent treatment thing at the facility really hurt.

"I understand why you did it, Cooper, but you have to know how much that hurt. When I lost Austin, I felt so alone. It took everything in me to keep moving, to keep living. I not only lost my brother but my best friend. By the time I was picked up, I hadn't talked to anyone in months. I was scared. No, not scared. Terrified. I had no idea what was going to happen to me." I pause. I want my next point to come through loud and clear. "Then, I was tortured. And beaten." The more I talk, the worse he looks. "From there, I was paraded in front of who knows how many men completely naked. I had to watch the men grope themselves while staring at me. Then the fight, where two men died trying to "win" me. Those men died because of me! Do you get that? If I hadn't been there, they would still be alive!"

"Honey, that wasn't your fault," he says trying to soothe me.

"Yes, it was! They died because they wanted me! How can you say it wasn't my fault?" I ask, my eyes starting to fill up with tears.

He pulls me over and into his lap. He holds me tight, rubbing one hand up and down my back. "Baby. Look at me," he says, turning my head so that I have to look into his eyes. "Those deaths, they're on me. Those men didn't have to die, you're right. All I had to do was win. When Devon got the knife, I knew if I hung back, those two idiots would kill each other, and I wouldn't have to do anything. Stone killed Devon, Cass, not you. And I killed Stone. I had to. I knew if I didn't but still won, he would keep coming for you. That's just how he was. So those deaths are on me, not you."

I guess, in a way, he's right. But I know that part of me will always feel responsible.

"Agree to disagree," I say. "But that's not really the point."

"So, then what is the point?" he asks me, pushing my hair away from my face.

"The point is, that when I finally got into the cell with you, the man who killed to have me, you completely dismissed me. From the moment that you volunteered, I felt you were different. You came off as someone who would protect me, who would make sure I was safe. And I did feel safe with you. But to be completely ignored, after months on my own, after losing the only other person on this planet who mattered to me, it was like a knife to the heart," I say, a few tears leaking down my cheek.

He puts his head down for a minute, his chin to his chest. He stays like that for a few minutes. I hate to admit it, but part of me is glad that my pain hurts him. I want him to know how it feels. But the other part of me hates that he is in pain. I am just about to tell him that when he picks his head up. I see a tear running down his cheek. He leans forward and rests his forehead against mine.

"Baby, I can't even begin to tell you how sorry I am. I had no idea that you were feeling any of that. I mean I knew you missed Austin, but I didn't even stop to think about how alone you were feeling. You must think I am an asshole," he says.

"Well, not an asshole, per se. Just a little bit of an ass," I tease.

This, at least, earns a smile from him.

"What can I do? How can I make it up to you?" he asks.

I giggle internally at his eagerness. It says a lot about him that he feels so bad, which makes him that much more attractive. But in all seriousness, hurt that deep doesn't just go away. I'm not saying that I am going to hold this against him forever, but I do need some time.

"Nothing. There's nothing you can do but give me time," I say.

"Ah. The old, time heals all wounds thing," he says.

"Yeah. Something like that."

He pushes some of my hair that fell loose back behind my ears. He stares into my eyes for a few moments. He finally leans forward and kisses me on the forehead.

"Well, what do you say we head back inside and get some sleep? We have a long day tomorrow and we'll need the rest," he says.

"Long day? Doing what?" I ask.

"We are going to stock up, and head to my group's headquarters."

"Where is that? And where are we right now?" I ask, not really having any idea where we are or where the facility was located.

"The facility was in Washington, D.C. Right now, we are a little bit south of that, in Virginia."

"So, I guess I was off course trying to get to your cabin," I say.

He looks up at me and smirks. "Actually, no. From what I was told, they found you at my cabin," he says, sounding proud.

"That was your cabin I was staying at!"

"Yeah. You made it there on your own. I guess all of Austin's training paid off," he says with a smile.

Huh. I really thought I was in the wrong place. The compass and map that I was using weren't top-of-the-line. Our good equipment was in Austin's bag. There were no personal items in the cabin to suggest that it was his. I smile, proud of myself.

"Well, someone is proud of herself," he says, standing up with me still in his arms. Talk about sexy, this man is pure muscle. He must notice my blush because he smirks and wiggles his eyebrows at me.

I punch him in the shoulder.

"Shut up."

12

Confessions

We make our way back into the cave and I go over to my bag to grab some other clothes. After spending the day running, these clothes feel pretty dirty and smelly. I want something fresh to wear, not that any of my other clothes are clean.

"Here," Cooper says, handing me a pair of sweatpants and a hoodie. "They are spares that they left in the cave just in case. These should fit you."

"How do you know they will fit?" I ask.

"I pay very close attention to you, beautiful." This makes me blush. "Oh, and take this," he says, handing me a small bag. "It's body wipes, so you can clean up a bit."

I smile and turn around heading over to the dark corner.

"Turn your back so I can get dressed," I say. "And no peeking!"

"First of all, Cass. I have already seen everything that you have to offer. And not a single part of me is complaining. Second, do you have any idea how many opportunities I have had to peek? Between showers and the toilet in the cell, I could have seen you about ten times a day."

I scowl at him.

"I never peeked, Cass. Not once. And the only reason I looked the first time, is because I didn't want my eyes closed should something happen, and I needed to protect you."

Why does everything that this man says make sense? It's so aggravating.

Because I am a mature adult, I stick my tongue out at him before I turn around to get changed. I hear him laughing.

Once dressed, I make my way back over to him and see that he has changed into a pair of cotton pants and a long sleeve shirt. Which, by the way, leaves nothing to the imagination. You can make out every line and curve of his muscles and I have to check myself to make sure I am not drooling.

He is in the process of unfolding something. A cot. I smile, thankful that I am not going to have to sleep on the ground.

"One cot?" I ask.

"Well, there is a second. But if you would rather cuddle with me, I won't set it up," he says, smirking the entire time.

"Two will be fine thanks," I say, walking over to put my dirty clothes in my bag.

I spend a few minutes brushing my hair, because yes, thankfully I do actually have a brush. After I pull it up into a messy bun on the top of my head, I see that he has finished setting up the cots with some sleeping bags. They are right next to each other, touching on one side which makes me raise my eyebrows at him in question.

"I'd rather us be close, just in case something happens," he says in explanation.

I just shake my head and start to sit down on the cot closest to me.

"Not that one, sweetheart. You sleep in the other one," he says.

"I'm sorry, I didn't realize you had already called dibs on this one," I say.

"It's not that at all. I just want to sleep closer to the entrance of the cave. I want you behind me so that I can protect you if I need to."

I just smile at that. What else can I do? I have a feeling that no matter how long I try to hold onto my anger, he is just going to needle his way into my heart faster than I would like.

We both lay down in our sleeping bags and get settled in for the night. He lowers the light of the lantern so that it is pitch black. The cool night breeze is making its way in from outside and I find myself shivering a little. It's late fall, so it's starting to get really cold at night around here. We didn't start a fire because there is no ventilation in the cave for the smoke. We don't really have any other options so the sleeping bags will just have to do. After a few minutes, he breaks the silence.

"Cass? Can I ask you something?"

"Sure," I say.

He pauses as if gathering the courage to ask. "Did you mean what you said to me back at the facility?"

"Which thing? If I remember correctly, I said a lot," I say, partially teasing.

I'm not sure if he doesn't pick up on my teasing or if he is being really serious right now because he just continues. "The part where you said where you have really come to care for me," he says quietly.

I don't answer right away, not really sure where he is going with this. To be completely honest, yes, I do really care for him. In fact, I think I might actually love him after everything that he has done for me. But I definitely don't want to admit that. At least not yet.

"Yes. I meant it," I say, rolling over to face him.

"Do you think?" he starts, but then stops. "Never mind."

"No. Do I think what?"

"Do you think you could ever love me?"

Shit.

"Do we really need to talk about this right now? I mean, I am freezing over here," I say, trying to distract him.

"You're cold?" he asks, immediately going into protector mode.

"I'm surprised you can't hear my teeth chattering over there," I say sarcastically.

I hear rustling and a zipper. Before I know it, he has unzipped my sleeping bag and pulled me to my feet.

"What are you doing?" I ask.

"Just give me a minute," he says.

After a few minutes, he tells me to lie down again. He has zipped our two sleeping bags together so that it is one big sleeping bag. I lay down, and he scoots in behind me, zipping us in together.

"Now wait a minute," I start, but he interrupts me.

"Just stop. I won't try anything. But if Austin taught you anything, it's that body heat is the best insulation in the cold."

He's right.

I roll over so that my back is to his front. He scoots forward so that he is spooning me and wraps his arm around my waist. It only takes a second for me to relax into him. I actually find myself inching back closer to him.

"This is nice," he says. I can feel him nuzzling my hair.

"Yeah, well don't get used to it. It's just for the night so that we stay warm," I say.

"Well, if you don't mind, I'm going to enjoy it while it lasts. It feels really good to have you in my arms finally. You don't know how many times I wish I could have crawled into that bed with you at the facility. I just wanted to hold you."

I don't reply, keeping my thoughts to myself. My thoughts are, yeah, me too.

It's quiet for a few minutes. Long enough that I think he may have fallen asleep. But he is definitely not sleeping.

"I just wanted to hold you," he whispers into my hair.

I find myself resting my hand over his arm that is wrapped around my waist. I draw little circles on his skin.

"Yes," I whisper, answering his earlier question quietly.

"Yes, what?" he asks, pulling me tighter.

"Just, yes," I say.

We lay silently, just holding each other. It's really nice. Nice enough that it distracts me from everything that is going on in the world right now. It doesn't take me long to doze off. Just as I am about to fall completely asleep, I hear him say one more thing.

"I love you, Cassidy."

13

On the Road Again

I awake to the smell of something wonderful. Coffee. I can't even remember the last time that I had any. I sit up and wipe the grogginess from my eyes.

"I was starting to wonder if you were ever going to wake up," Cooper says, walking over to me with a steaming cup.

"Please, please tell me that is coffee," I say, grabbing the cup out of his hands.

I hold the cup up to my nose and inhale deeply. I take my first sip and find myself moaning at the flavor. I know it has to be only instant coffee, but it is still the best thing I have tasted. I used to drink four to five cups a day. When everything went to shit, coffee wasn't on the list of priorities.

I look up at Cooper and find him staring at me.

"What?"

He swallows.

"Nothing," he says, shaking his head and turning back towards the table.

"No, what?" I push.

"I am trying really hard to give you time here, Cass. But if you keep moaning like that..." he trails off, leaving me to fill in the rest of his thought.

I blush. I find myself blushing around him a lot. I am a virgin, but I am not stupid. I know what he is saying.

"Sorry," I say sheepishly.

"Nothing to be sorry about. I'm just giving you fair warning," he says, smirking.

You know, there are times when I find his smirking extremely sexy, and others when I want to wipe it off his face with a swift kick to his junk.

I just shake my head at him and go over to my bag to grab some clothes for the day. Once I have everything that I need, I turn back around.

"So, where am I supposed to, uh, take care of business?" I ask him, realizing that I really need to pee.

He laughs.

"Well, we aren't exactly at the Hilton right now. I don't have a toilet, but I do have some toilet paper. You can go right outside behind a tree and do your thing. I'll stand by and keep an eye out for you."

"Fine. But no..."

"Peeking. Yeah, yeah. I know."

We head outside and I take care of business. I dress quickly because it is quite chilly out this morning. I put on some jeans and a hoodie, my hiking boots, and pull my hair back up into a ponytail. I scoop up my clothes and step around the tree.

"Beautiful as always, Cass," Cooper says. I shake my head.

"What's the plan for today, Coop?" I ask.

"Well, we are going to headquarters. It's going to take us a day to get there. If we keep up a good pace, we might make it there by tonight."

"Where is headquarters?"

"It's in Virginia, just a bit south of here, in Norfolk," he explains. "It's located on an Army base. The General who organized this group was stationed at that base when everything happened."

"And how, again, did you get hooked up with them?"

He smiles, but it doesn't reach his eyes.

"Let's go inside and get packed up. I'll explain while we are walking."

We head back inside the cave and fill our packs with supplies. Supplies being weapons, navigation equipment, food, and other necessities. I also throw in my personal items.

I take one last look around the cave to make sure that we aren't forgetting anything. He comes up behind me and places his hand on my shoulder.

"Ready?" he asks me.

I just nod. It's kind of nerve-racking, to not know what your future holds. Before everything happened, I had my life planned out, well, most of it. I was in graduate school. I had a good place to live, I had friends. I knew where my life was going. Now? Now, it's like I don't even know what will happen in the next hour, let alone the rest of my life. My life's goal has changed from becoming a therapist for children to just making it through the day.

We head outside to begin our hike when he turns to me.

"What's going on in that beautiful head of yours?" he asks me.

"Well, honestly, I was just thinking how everything has changed. I mean, before all this shit started, I knew exactly where my life was going. Now, I don't even know if I am going to survive from day to day. It's terrifying, to say the least."

"Cass, I would never let anything happen to you. You know that right?" he says, glancing back at me.

I just shrug my shoulders.

He stops, turns around, and comes right at me. He grabs my shoulders and makes me look right at him.

"No. That's not good enough. I promise, Cass. I will never, ever let anyone hurt you again. I need you to understand that," he says, very seriously.

"I know that you mean that Cooper. I really do. But honestly, can you really guarantee that? Can anyone really ever make that promise?"

"I can. Because... well, because I love you, Cass. I love you more than anything in the world and I would die if anything happened to you. Seriously. I don't think I would be able to go on without you," he says.

I laugh a little at his confession. "You can't mean that," I say.

"One of these days, Cass, I'm going to prove it to you. One of these days, you are going to realize that everything I am saying is true."

He lets go of me and turns back around. We begin walking again.

We are silent for a bit, both of us lost in thought, I'm guessing. I think about what he said. He has done nothing but try to convince me of his love since he began talking to me. It's thrilling, yet terrifying. I have never been in love before, so I don't know if what I am feeling for him is really love. But I do know that I truly care for him, deeply. But for him to tell me that he wouldn't be able to go on if something happened to me... That's just crazy. How could he love me that much?

The forest is loud. Leaves crunching under our feet, birds chirping. The wind is blowing at our backs. There isn't much foliage left on the trees at this point, being so far into the fall. I spend some time just taking it all in. I guess I have never really made myself look so hard at my surroundings. Austin always taught me that the first thing you should do in any situation is to take in your surroundings. I am looking around now, and really focusing on what could be out there. You never think about it, because honestly, who would, but there are so many places someone could be hiding, just waiting to ambush you. Probably not something I should focus on right now.

After a while, I break the silence. "So. You were going to explain how you met up with these guys," I say.

"Oh, yeah."

He walks a few steps before he starts his story. "A friend of mine and Austin's called me a few days after things went to hell. Trev knew that Aus and I were on leave. He told me that his General was organizing a group of men to help until things were figured out. He told me that all we would have to do was help the people that came to the base for protection. The General made it very clear that he was doing this on his own, and not as part of any type of governmental plan. Back in the beginning, the government panicked. Everyone knew that. They don't like to look like they don't know what they were doing, but just the fact that they couldn't explain what was going on, made people doubt them.

"No one knew what happened. No one. And because they couldn't explain anything, the government's first response was to try and "collect," if you will, all the remaining females for protection. They wanted the people to believe that they were going to be taken care of, even though there were so many questions. Unfortunately, by protect, they didn't mean protect. They meant research. They were desperate to figure out what was going on. They didn't want anyone else to get the answers before them, making them look the fools. The General got word of this and strongly disagreed. His wife and daughter had survived and the last thing he wanted to do was to turn them over for experimentation. I definitely can't blame the man. I would never be able to turn you in."

He pauses for a second as if gathering his thoughts.

"It took some convincing on Trev's part, but eventually, I agreed. My main concern was you and I didn't want this to take away from finding and protecting you. He convinced me that Austin would take care of you. This was after I had spoken to Austin and had made plans to meet at my cabin. I finally agreed but was upfront with them that you were my priority."

We walk for a little bit before he continues.

"Once I finally agreed, I had to make plans. I knew that it would take you two a while to make it to the cabin. So, before I went there, I went to the base to check things out. It seemed pretty straightforward. I originally wondered how this General could have taken command of a Governmental facility, but once I got there, it was pretty clear. They told me that all the soldiers were pulled out of there to look for survivors. They began turning any women's prisons throughout the country into research facilities. They had cells to hold people, and because it was a women's prison, they had the medical facilities with the right equipment. They brought in the rest. So, because most of the soldiers left to help with acquisitions, the base was pretty much vacant. The General remained and took command. He asked for volunteers to stay with him, only approaching those he knew he could trust. It all snowballed from there. They say that word of mouth is the best advertisement. Well, they're right. Word began to spread, and people began to come. Families with surviving women came. Women who were on their own came. But the worst, was when small children showed up. No parents, no protection. I'll never be able to explain how horrible a sight it was to see a child, completely broken, show up with no shoes, no food, and dirty beyond recognition. How they got there, I have no idea. But they were safe, and that's all that mattered.

"After a while, I realized that we really had no way of getting intel. I had a meeting with the General and suggested that we put plants in some of the facilities. People who we know we can trust and who can get us more information. So, we did. We sent our friends undercover. Not long after that, I received word from one of our men, that Austin had been picked up. He recognized him from a previous assignment. He knew that he and I were close, so he let me know. Austin told him that he had been picked up but that you were still out there. He provided the location of where he was picked up and the direction that you would have been headed. And, you know the rest."

I am silent for a bit after he finishes. When I finally find my voice, I really don't know what to say.

"Wow. That's a lot to take in."

He laughs.

"Honestly, at this point, there is nothing that surprises me," he says.

"So, no one really has any idea what happened?" I ask.

"Well, there are some theories. There is a pastor at the base who was trying to convince everyone that this is an act of God. That God was punishing us for our actions by taking away our ability to reproduce. But that doesn't make complete sense because there are women who survived. You would think that he would have wiped out all women, and not just some if that is the case."

"I'm not a religious person so I really can't say that I agree with that theory," I say.

"Yeah, me neither. But there was another theory floating around, as well," he says.

"And what's that?" I'm almost afraid to hear.

He takes a deep breath. "A man who came in with his wife and two daughters who survived started spreading his theory. He apparently worked as a geneticist at a huge pharmaceutical plant. He said that he believed this was an act of terrorism. He believed that someone found a way to, I guess, poison women so that only those with certain genetic markers would survive. He wanted to start drawing blood from survivors to test his theory. He was beginning his research when I left."

"That's a scary thought. That this is the result of some evil mastermind," I say, half joking.

"Yeah. And if they can do this, what else are they capable of," he continues my thoughts.

We fall silent, both thinking about those implications.

14

Almost There

We spend the next few hours just talking about our lives. I think our earlier conversation was a bit too heavy, so we moved on to lighter topics. He asked me about college, I asked him about his childhood.

He grew up in the system, his mother having abandoned him on the steps of a police station right after he was born. He has no idea who either of his parents is, but he said that he grew up in a nice home with great foster parents. He was never adopted. When he graduated from high school and aged out of the foster home, he decided to enlist and become a Marine. He thought that was the next logical step being that he didn't have any money for college.

We break for lunch and snacks at different points throughout the day. He thinks we are making great time and should be there by dark. It isn't until later in the day that he gets into the nitty gritty.

"So, have you had many boyfriends?" he asks, glancing back at me nervously.

I laugh. "Oh yeah. Tons. I went out with a different guy every night," I tease him.

He stops and turns to look at me. There is anger in his eyes.

"Ok, ok. Calm down. No, I didn't have a lot of boyfriends. I dated a few times, but nothing serious," I say, trying to calm him down.

"So, no relationships?" he asks.

I smile. "No. No one I wanted to spend more than one date with," I say. "How about you? What's your story?"

"Nothing to tell. A few dates here and there. Usually while on leave. But nothing serious," he says, looking at the ground.

"Why do I think you aren't telling me the truth?" I ask suspiciously.

He coughs and clears his throat. He looks nervous.

"Look, Cooper. I know you are older than me. I also know that men are different from women in that they see sex as a more casual thing. It's ok that you've... that you're..." I can't finish that sentence because it honestly angers me to think of him with another woman.

He sits down on a fallen log and pats the spot next to him. I go over and sit down.

"I'm sorry," he says.

This shocks me. "For what?" I ask incredulously.

"I feel like I cheated on you. I had a few moments of weakness. I was feeling low like I would never get my chance with you. I felt pathetic. I was in love with a woman I had never met. I caved."

He says this all, bent over, elbows on his knees, and head in his hands. I honestly don't know what to do so I gently place a hand on his shoulder.

"Cooper, we hadn't even met. We aren't even together now," I say, which causes him to whip his head up and look at me.

"Oh," is all he says.

He stands up and turns around, ready to start back on our trek.

"No, Cooper, wait!"

He stops, picking up a rock and throwing it into the woods, as hard as he can.

I get up and go over to him. "Look. I know how you feel about me. And I think I know how I feel about you. But it's not like we can go out on a date or whatever. I mean, what is this? What do you expect to happen?" I ask.

Apparently, this is the wrong thing to say. His face changes to a mask of nothing.

"Nothing. I expect nothing," he says dryly. "Come on, we have to keep moving. We are almost there."

"Cooper," I start, but he just starts walking.

He is done with this conversation. And for some reason, that hurts.

I wasn't trying to say that I don't want him. I'm just... I don't even know. I just know that I care about him more than I ever thought possible. But with everything going on right now, is it smart to start a relationship? If anything, I feel like it would make things worse. I worry that he would get hurt, or even worse, killed, trying to protect me. He would be focused on me and not what he is supposed to be doing. But there is no way to explain this to him. And I don't think he wants to hear it right now anyway.

15

Headquarters

We walk in silence the rest of the way. I can tell that he is mad at me. He still turns around to help me if we need to climb over something, but his touch doesn't linger as it used to before he was mad. I don't really know what to say to him to make it better so, I just stay silent. I hate that he is mad at me. This seems like a teeter-totter – I was mad at him, and he's mad at me. A vicious cycle of anger.

Just after dusk, we arrive at the base. It's a large area surrounded by a tall fence with barbed wire around the top. I can make out a lot of vehicles, mostly jeeps and trucks, all in camouflage. I see lights in the distance, probably the living quarters, or maybe even offices, I have no idea. I have never been on an Army base before.

We walk up to a guard shack. The man inside comes out and salutes Cooper.

"Staff Sergeant Matthews. It's good to see you, sir," a young man, probably around my age, says to Cooper.

"Hunter. At ease, kid. Good to see you, too," Cooper says.

"Is this her? Did you find her?" the kid asks.

"Yeah. This is Cassidy Daniels. Cass, this is Private Tom Hunter."

I shake his hand, doing the whole, nice-to-meet-you-thing.

"I'm so glad you found her, Coop. I know how worried you were," Tom starts but is cut off by Coop.

"Yeah. Is the General here?"

He looks taken aback.

"Yes, sir. I can let him know you are here," Tom says, handing Coop a set of keys. "Take the Jeep. He's in his office."

We say our goodbyes to Tom, with Cooper promising to catch up with him later. We get in the Jeep and Cooper heads towards the lights in the distance. I can't take the silent treatment anymore.

"Cooper, will you please talk to me?" I laugh to myself. How many times have I said that before?

"What's to talk about, Cass? You made your point. I won't bother you anymore. I got you here, you are safe. Now we can go our separate ways," he says without any emotion.

"What! So, that's it? You're just going to walk away?" I ask, angry that he is being like this.

"Sure. I promised Austin if anything were to happen to him that I would make sure you are safe. I've done my job. Now I can move on and help in the fight."

"Well, what if I want to help, too?" I ask. He laughs.

"Uh, no. That would defeat the whole keeping you safe thing," he says, shitting on my idea.

"Well, you aren't the boss of me. I'll just have to talk to this General and volunteer for missions. I'm sure they are looking for all the help they can get," I say defiantly.

He growls. "Do whatever you want, Cassidy. I couldn't care less."

"You know what? You can be a real ass, Cooper Matthews! And I know that you don't mean that. Just because I didn't say I love you back, doesn't mean..." I trail off.

He slams on the brakes and looks over at me. We are stopped in the middle of the road. There are lights lining the road and the interior lights of the Jeep are giving off a bit, but all I can see is the anger on his face.

"Doesn't mean what, Cass? Doesn't mean what? Say it if you mean it," he says.

I blush and look down. I don't want to have this conversation, especially not now.

"Just drop it, please. I'm not... I can't."

"Can't, or won't, Cass? Which is it? It's a big difference. At least it is for me," he says sadly.

A tear falls, even though I was fighting like hell to prevent its escape.

"I care for you, Cooper. So much." I say, trying to find the courage to finish. I turn to look at him. He fights me when I try to pick up his hand. "Cooper, I'm afraid."

This softens his face. "Cass," he starts.

"No. Let me get this out." I pause, gathering the courage to tell him what I'm thinking. "I'm so afraid. I've lost everyone that I love, Coop. Everyone. I'm scared of opening myself up to that hurt again. I can't even imagine how much it would hurt if I lost you, too. I've never felt this way before. The only type of love that I have known is the love that I have for my family. What I feel for you, is so much more than that. I don't want you risking your life protecting me. I don't want anything to happen to you... because of me. I couldn't live with myself. So, I can't do this with you. Not yet. If things were different, I wouldn't hesitate."

Well, there it is. I laid it all out there.

He doesn't say anything. He just sits there, letting me hold his hand. I can't even say that he is holding mine back.

Finally, he sighs. He then squeezes my hand and leans over to kiss me on the cheek.

"I'll wear you down, Cass. You won't have a choice but to admit that you love me," he says.

I am dumbfounded. I thought for sure that he would be angry. But apparently, all I did was give him incentive.

Oh, boy. What did I just do?

• • • •

We make it to a parking lot, and he pulls into an empty spot. The building in front of us says "Administration." I guess we are heading in to see the General.

We both get out, leaving our bags behind. He holds the door open for me and we make our way inside. There is a security desk about ten feet inside the door. The man behind it stands at attention when he sees Cooper.

"At ease," Coop says. "The General should be expecting us."

"I'll let him know you are here, Staff Sergeant. You can head down and have a seat outside his office."

He nods, and we make our way up some stairs and down a long hallway. I have to admit, it's kind of weird to see people saluting Cooper and calling him sir. To me, he's just Cooper.

There is a woman sitting at a desk outside of a set of double wooden doors. She smiles when she sees us.

"He's expecting you. Go right in," she says sweetly.

Cooper opens the door, and we walk in. The office is huge. Bookshelves line every wall, and they are filled with books of all shapes and sizes. The entire office seems to be made of mahogany. It makes me afraid to touch anything. I guess the General is into weapons as there are many different types of rifles and handguns mounted on any spare wall space around the office.

The General, himself, is a tall man with gray hair and dark eyes. He has a muscular build. He looks to be in his mid-fifties or so. He stands when he sees Cooper.

"Staff Sergeant Matthews. So good to see you, son," he says as Cooper salutes him. "At ease."

Cooper nods, then makes his way over to the General. He pulls Cooper in for a hug, which surprises me.

"I was getting worried that we might not see you again. It's been months," the General says.

Cooper looks over at me and smiles.

"Yeah. There were a few complications, but it all worked out. General Michael McConnell, I'd like to introduce you to Cassidy Daniels. Cass, this is General McConnell."

I go over to him and shake his hand. He has a soothing smile. I would expect someone of his power to be intimidating.

"Tell me everything," he says to Cooper.

We take a seat at the chairs in front of his desk and Cooper tells our tale. He leaves out some of the more embarrassing and intimate moments, focusing only on the practical information.

"Cassidy, what can you tell me about the employees on the medical side? Did you get any names or ranks?" the General asks me gently.

I look over at Cooper, and he nods his head, telling me it's ok to give him the information. He trusts this man, that much is obvious.

"I'm sorry but the only name that I got was of the head doctor, the one who tortured me," I say. Cooper's hands tighten into fists at this statement. I reach over and put my hand over his. He takes my hand and begins rubbing circles on the back of my hand with his thumb. I guess he knows that I need his strength right now. This isn't exactly a memory that I want to relive.

"His name is Dr. Anderson. I didn't get a first name." I go on to describe my time with him. I tell him everything about the torture, the testing, and the preparations for the presentation. Everything. As embarrassing as it is, I unload it all.

He sits quietly, listening to all that I have to say.

"Hmm. Anderson. I wonder," he says, rubbing his jaw and thinking.

"You aren't thinking Dr. Garrett Anderson, are you?" Cooper asks.

"I am, actually," General McConnell says.

"Who is he?" I ask the obvious question.

Cooper sighs, squeezing my hand.

"He was the President's top Medical Adviser. Off the records, of course. I know you are thinking that he is not the one that was on the news for the President after everything started. No, that was the official Medical Advisor to the President. Dr. Garrett Anderson is a different type of adviser. He does things a little differently. He uses, let's just say, more direct methods of getting his research done."

"Torture. You mean, torture," I say blandly.

General McConnell gives me a sad look.

"I'm so sorry that you had to go through that, Cassidy. Truly. But if it is any kind of consolation, you have just provided me with some very important information."

"And what is that General?" I ask.

"Please, Cassidy. Call me Mike. And what you just told me proves something that I have suspected all along. That the facility that you were in, is their main facility. They wouldn't put Anderson anywhere insignificant. I would suspect that he is overseeing their entire operation. That all other facilities report to him."

"General, if you don't mind. Do you have any other information on Austin?" Cooper interrupts.

"Wait, what? You have information on Austin?" I ask excitedly.

"Cassidy," Cooper says calmly. "I told you a while ago that the only reason I knew where you were is because I had a guy getting me information from Austin at the facility that he is in."

Holy fucking shit. I am an idiot. I was so focused on what was going on and who Cooper was, that I didn't stop to think about what everything meant.

"Oh my God! I can't believe I missed that! Is he ok? Is he here?" I ramble so fast I can barely get the words out.

"Whoa, whoa. Cass. I wondered why you never asked. You were so focused on other things, I guess it never occurred to you. But it's ok," Cooper says to comfort me.

I guess I start shaking, tears are falling, and I am suddenly freezing. Shock.

Cooper pulls me over into his lap and holds me tight. He nods at Mike to answer mine and his questions.

"He's ok, Cassidy. I assure you. No, he is not here. But we know exactly where he is, as Cooper said. We are in the process of planning the takedown of the facility and getting him out. He's one of the

Marine's best, and we definitely want him here safely so that he can help us continue our mission," Mike says.

"I want to help. I want to go when they take it down. I have to," I say.

"Easy, Cass. Easy. Let me look at the plans and figure some things out. I'll let you know if there is any way for you to help," Cooper says.

"No. I'm going. And you can't stop me," I say, standing up from his lap defiantly. There is no way in hell I am letting them stop me.

I hear Mike chuckle. "You are going to have your hands full with this one, Coop."

"Don't I know it," he mumbles.

16

Roommates

We finish up with the General and say our goodbyes. He says he will see us both at the next planning session tomorrow, which causes Cooper to growl. I'm sure it's the fact that Mike mentioned he would see both of us there and not just Cooper. I guess he realizes that I am stubborn and will get my way no matter what.

Cooper is quiet as he drives us over to the housing buildings. We were told to go to Building 5. After grabbing our bags, we head inside and check in. The young man at the desk tells us we are in room 1010.

"Uh. There should be two rooms," I say.

"Beg your pardon, ma'am. But I have you both in the same room. Staff Sergeant Matthews request," he says.

I turn to Cooper and scowl. He just smiles and winks at me.

I grab the keys from the kid and storm away. I hear Cooper say something under his breath which I'm sure is "told you I'd wear you down."

I open the door and see the small room that looks almost like my freshman dorm room. Two small single beds, one against each wall, two small dressers, and that's it. Functional, I guess. At least there are two beds.

I walk over to the one on the right and plop down. It's a soft mattress with clean sheets. To be perfectly honest, I would be happy with just the mattress right now. I'm exhausted.

"Don't worry. We can push the beds together," Cooper says, dropping onto the other bed.

"I'm good, thanks," I say sarcastically.

He smirks. Remember when I said that sometimes I want to wipe the smirks off his face with a swift kick to his junk? Yeah, fighting the urge.

I go over to the dresser and see that there are clean clothes in the drawers. I smile. I have never been so happy to see clean clothes in my life. I don't even care that they aren't mine. I grab some yoga pants and a long sleeve shirt. I open the top drawer and see something amazing. Underwear. And bras! I have hit the jackpot.

With my hands full of clothing, I ask Cooper where the bathrooms are. He grabs some clothes for himself and tells me to follow him.

We walk down the hallway to the end. There are apparently shared bathrooms in each hall. Co-ed bathrooms. Yikes. We make our way inside. Due to it being so late in the day, the bathroom is empty. I walk towards the showers and step inside the last one in the row. Cooper takes the one next to me.

"Let me know if you need me to do your back," he says before he disappears with a wink.

I turn the water on and let it warm up while I take my clothes off. I step in the shower and just let the water roam over me for a second. I look up and see a shelf with shampoos and conditioners, body washes, and soaps. I smile thankfully to whoever stocked the showers. I make quick work of washing my hair, not wanting to linger too long with Cooper right next to me.

When I go to pick up the body wash, I stop cold. It's the same kind that they gave me to use at the facility, right before my presentation. I drop it like it's hot coal and gasp. I back away until my back hits the wall and find myself sliding down to the floor. I pull my knees up into my chest and wrap my hands around them. Before I know it, I am sobbing. Not a cute little quiet girl sob. This is an all-out, ugly snot-filled sob. I can't control it. I feel like I have been transported back to that place and I can't escape. The walls are closing in, and I feel like I am about to be "presented" again. I am in that facility and there is no escape.

"Cass," Cooper says from right outside my curtain. "Cass. What's going on? Are you ok?"

I am too worked up to even answer.

The curtain moves and I see Cooper standing there with a towel wrapped around his waist. Once he sees me, he is immediately at my side.

He shuts the water off, sits on the floor next to me, and pulls me into his lap. He just holds me, allowing me to slobber all over his chest. I've never been what I would call a crier. But for some reason, I guess everything just hit me. I was tortured. I was experimented on. I was violated.

It takes a while, but I finally get myself calmed down. Without looking at him, I whisper, "I'm so sorry."

"Baby, you have nothing to be sorry for. But you have to tell me what happened? Did someone hurt you?"

"No. I'm ok. Just a bad memory," I say, kicking the body wash away from us.

He sees me kick the bottle. "What did that body wash do to you?"

I take a deep breath, knowing that this is going to sound silly. "It was the same body wash that they gave me in the facility. It just made me feel like I was back there. I know it's stupid. It's just body wash," I say, feeling stupid.

He puts his fingers under my chin and lifts me up to look at him. I have wet hair stuck to me, tears running down my face, and I'm sure that I look a mess. Without even looking, I know that my cheeks are blotchy.

"You are still and will always be, the most gorgeous woman I have ever seen," Cooper says, knowing where my thoughts are as always. This man... "You are not stupid. I wish I could take it all away, Cass. I wish there was a way to go back in time and prevent you from having to go through all of that. But as cheesy as it sounds, I truly believe that what doesn't kill you, makes you stronger. You are the most beautiful woman, and yet still the biggest pain in my ass. But you are also the strongest, most amazing woman that I have ever met. Don't make me remind you how much I love you. Don't make me do it," he teases.

"I don't deserve you," I say quietly.

"Hey, now. Don't say that. It's me who doesn't deserve you. I'm just a stupid guy, well, extremely handsome, stupid guy, well, let's not forget about the many muscles and quick wit... wait, where was I going with this," he says, all the while smiling.

"Just shut up you, incredibly handsome, muscled-filled hunk of mine. Shut up and let me finish showering so we can get some sleep," I say.

He laughs as he grabs my towel so that I can cover myself before we get up. Once standing, he wipes the damp hair away from my face and kisses me on the forehead.

"Ok, beautiful. Finish your shower while I finish jerking off to the thought of you naked," he says as I punch him in the shoulder.

"Kidding, kidding," he laughs. "But seriously, I'm here if you need me."

I lean up and kiss him on the cheek. "Thanks."

He winks at me as he turns to leave. He, of course, flashes me his ass, because the tiny towels they have here are not big enough to cover all of him. I see his shoulder shaking as he walks away, making me realize that he is aware that he is flashing me. At least it gives me something good to think about while I finish my shower.

After getting dressed, I open the curtain to find Cooper standing guard right in front of my stall. It makes me smile. He's ready to go to war to protect me from my own memories.

We make our way back to our room. After brushing my hair and pulling it up on top of my head, I turn around to find Cooper already snug in his bed. I know I rolled my eyes at him at the thought of sleeping in the same bed again, but I honestly don't think I could sleep without his arms around me.

"Um, Coop," I say quietly, looking over at him. I have my hands in front of me and I am playing with a string coming off the bottom of my shirt.

He smiles at me. Without saying a word, he gets up, pushes the beds together, and crawls back in. He turns to face me, scooting back to make roo,m and holds the covers up for me to get in. I make my way over to him and crawl in. I don't waste time backing up so that I am pressed against his front. He wraps his arms around me so that I am using his huge bicep as my pillow and his other arm is wrapped around my middle. I pull the covers up so that we are both covered and settle in.

I drop my one hand down to wrap around the hand around my middle. My other hand goes up to play with the fingers of his right hand, the one I'm currently using as my pillow. We lay in silence for a while, just holding each other.

"Thank you, Cooper. Thank you for always being there," I say, squeezing his hand.

He doesn't respond immediately, making me think he has fallen asleep.

Then I hear, "slowly wearing you down, Cass." And I smile yet again.

17

Planning the Next Takedown

I wake up alone the next morning and am immediately angry. He'd better not have gone to the planning session without me. I throw the covers off and jump up. Before I get out of bed, I find a folded piece of paper on his pillow.

Cass,

Don't get your panties in a bunch. I didn't go to the planning session without you. I know that's what you were thinking. I went to grab us breakfast before we had to leave. Get yourself dressed and I will be back in a few.

Eternally yours,

Coop

Well, that is unexpected. I figured he would do anything to keep me from this meeting.

I get up and get dressed, grabbing another pair of yoga pants a hoodie, and my hiking boots, not knowing where today will take us. Just as I am tying my second boot, the door opens.

Coop comes in holding a box and some travel mugs filled with, if my nose is correct, coffee. I stand up and he immediately runs his eyes up and down my body, smiling appreciatively.

"Well, if this is what I have to look forward to each morning," he trails off.

"Ok. What did you bring me for breakfast?" I ask, changing the subject and rolling my eyes.

He comes over and sets the box down. When he opens it, my mouth immediately begins to water. Donuts. Very large, chocolate-covered donuts. My absolute favorite. Just when I think it can't get any better, he hands me the travel mug.

"Gourmet coffee. Hazelnut, with two creams and three sugars," he says, extremely proud of himself.

"Nice, stalker. But thanks," I say.

We both eat a donut, ok, I eat two, then we head out with our travel mugs.

"The meeting starts in about fifteen minutes. I want to get there early to introduce you to some of my brothers," Cooper says as we walk.

We make it to the building and go through what seems like a maze of hallways, finally reaching a meeting room with a very large wooden table in the center. There are about ten men seated around the table. When they see us enter, they all stand up.

Cooper goes over to the three guys standing on the right. After he does the whole bro-hug thing with all three of them, he turns to me.

"Cass, I'd like to introduce you to Simon, Al, and Teddy. We served together," he says. "Guys, this... this is Cassidy Daniels."

He says it like he is introducing them to someone of great importance. But I'm just me.

Each of them shakes my hand firmly as any Marine would.

I laugh.

"What's up?" Cooper asks, looking at me like I've lost it.

"Al, Simon, and Teddy, right? Like Alvin, Simon, and Theodore? I'm going to call you three the chipmunks," I say.

They just look at me for a second with blank faces before we all break out in hysterical laughter.

"Holy shit! How did I never think of that before?" Cooper says loudly.

The chipmunks are laughing, hard. Within seconds, they start singing in high-pitched voices, the theme song for Alvin and the Chipmunks.

"You never cease to amaze me. No wonder I love you so much," he says, kissing me on the side of the head.

The door jumps open and General McConnel walks in. It immediately falls silent as all the men in the room stand at attention.

In unison, they shout, "Good morning, General."

"At ease, men. Good morning," Mike says. Then he looks at me. "Good morning to you too, Cassidy."

We all take our seats, and the meeting begins. One man, who I learn is Staff Sergeant Steve Overton, describes their current situation.

"Ziggy, uh, Private Dave Zigman, is stationed at the facility in West Virginia. It's in Franklin in Pendleton County. He's provided all kinds of pertinent information including guard schedules, shift change procedures, cell locations, and occupant numbers. We know exactly where Staff Sergeant Daniels is located. We did some research and found some schematics of the building. We believe we can take it down with strategically timed explosives. We time our extraction with the detonations, and we can minimize casualties. From what we understand, there is minimal staff present in the hospital. They only bring staff in when they have a new female. At this point in time, they do not have any females in the facility. We are looking at forty-seven male prisoners, eight guards, six of whom Ziggy believes will come with us, and one person who he classified as administrative."

"Who do we have that can work the explosives?" the General asks.

The chipmunks raise their hands in unison.

"We are quite skilled in that area, sir," Teddy says. "We can handle the planning and execution on that side."

"Perfect. Who is working extraction?" he asks.

To my dismay, Cooper and two other men raise their hands.

"No," I say without thinking.

"Cass. We'll talk about this later," Coop warns. "Sorry for the interruption, sir."

"No, it's ok. What are you thinking, Cassidy?" Mike asks me.

Realizing that all eyes are on me right now is a bit unsettling. Cooper looks at me with pleading eyes, trying to silently tell me that we will discuss this later.

"I apologize, General. It's nothing," I say.

He smiles at me with understanding.

"Cassidy, I know you are concerned for Cooper's life, but you don't need to be. This is what he does. This is what he has been trained to do, and he is very skilled at what he does. And to be perfectly honest, there isn't anyone else I would want to complete this mission. He will ensure your brother's safety. Not only because he is your brother, but because it is his best friend and because it is his job. It is ingrained in everything that he is, to never fail. I know that he will complete this mission with utmost efficiency and swiftness," Mike reassures me.

I find myself embarrassed for my little outburst. Cooper reaches over and grabs my hand. I'm sure this isn't something he should be doing in front of a General in an official meeting, but I appreciate it. He nods at me as if agreeing with the General.

"Thank you, Mike," I say.

The meeting continues for the next couple of hours. Plans are made, and timing is set. It seems like everything should go down like clockwork. The only thing that is never mentioned, is my part.

Just as they are about to wrap up, I raise my hand, which earns a few chuckles.

"Cassidy, it's not that kind of meeting. If you have something to add, you can just say it," Mike says.

"Um, sir, I was just wondering what my part is. How can I help in the plan?" I ask.

Everyone falls silent. They all look at Cooper, who reaches over and picks up my hand.

"Cass, you'll be here at the base, waiting for us. I can't risk you getting hurt. I just can't," Cooper says.

I tear my hand out of his and stand up.

"No! This is my brother we are talking about! You can't stop me from being there. It's not fair. I need to be there. What if something goes wrong and that is my last chance to see him, to talk to him? You can't take that chance away from me," I say.

Cooper stands and pulls me into his arms. He is rubbing his hands up and down my back trying to soothe me. Whispering words of love and apology into my ear.

"I can go with her in a separate vehicle. We can hang back as backup if needed. I will protect her, stay with her the whole time, and make sure she is safe. That way she can be there, but be out of harm's way," I hear someone say in a rush.

I turn to see a man about my age looking right at me.

"Gunner, why would you do that?" Cooper asks.

Gunner, who is about my height with dark hair and brown eyes, looks at me.

"Staff Sergeant Daniels is the only reason I am standing here today. He believed in me, when no one else did, not even me. I had just been assigned to his group, having barely made it out of basic. I mean look at me. I'm not your typical Marine. I'm barely five foot six. I'm not built like a freight train, like Staff Sergeant Matthews or the other guys. Daniels helped me see my value, my worth. And, he was always talking about you, ma'am," Gunner says.

"Oh, please don't call me ma'am. Makes me feel old. I'm just Cassidy," I say, which earns a laugh from everyone.

"Well, Cassidy, he was always talking about you. I know how much he loves you. I know that he would want you to be there," he says.

I look over at Cooper, trying to tell how he feels about this plan, but his face is blank.

"Well?" I ask him.

He narrows his eyes at Gunner.

"You will keep her safe? No matter what? You're willing to give up your life to protect her if that's what it comes down to?" he says, sounding threatening.

"Yes, sir," Gunner says, without hesitation.

Cooper looks over at the General, who nods his approval. Cooper scowls.

"If anything happens to her..." he threatens.

"It will be fine, Coop. I promise. I won't get in the way. I just need to be there, please," I say.

He just nods, leaning down and kissing my forehead.

The meeting ends and everyone stands. Small groups break off to discuss the meeting and I make my way over to Gunner.

"I can't thank you enough," I say to him. "I just wanted to officially introduce myself. I'm Cassidy Daniels."

He shakes my hand. "Troy Gunnerson, but everyone calls me Gunner. But you already know that I guess," he says, blushing. "Your brother is a great man."

"I'm sure he is very proud of you. And I know that he will appreciate what you are doing."

I feel a presence behind me and know without looking that it is Cooper.

"Sir, I will protect her with my life, I swear," Gunner says.

"At ease, kid. I know." Cooper wraps his arms around my middle, pulling me back into him. I know that he is making a point to Gunner, that I am off-limits. "This woman means everything to me, and I mean it when I say that if something happens to her, I will come after you."

"My goodness, Cooper. Take it easy. Nothing is going to happen to me," I say, trying to squirm out of his hold.

"Come on, Cass. Let's go get some lunch," he says, pulling me away.

I pull my hand out of Cooper's and walk over to Gunner. I give him a quick hug and thank him again.

"I'm sure I'll see you soon," I say, as Cooper pulls me away again. I don't stop him this time.

We make our way back through the maze of hallways until we are outside. He doesn't go to the Jeep, though. He keeps pulling me past the parking lot and over to a set of benches. He takes me over to the furthest one and motions for me to sit down. I expect him to sit next to me, but he doesn't. He just starts pacing back and forth, extremely agitated.

"Cooper. Talk to me. Where is your head right now?" I ask, pleading with him.

He stops pacing for a second to look at me. What I see in his eyes scares the hell out of me. He looks like someone just, well, like someone just killed his best friend, or ran over his puppy. It's hard to tell.

He starts pacing again so I stand up and get right in his way, to stop him. I put one hand on each side of his face and force him to look at me.

"Talk to me."

He just looks at me for a few moments. He then reaches up and places his hands over mine. "I don't want you anywhere near there, not after everything that you went through. It's not that I doubt Gunner, because I don't. I know of him through Austin. He talked about him a lot. It's just that it's not me protecting you. I won't be there if something happens."

"I get it. I do. But you have to realize that there will be moments in our lives when you won't always be there. You have to trust me. You have to trust other people to help. I don't want to lose you either. Did you think of that? I don't want you going in there. What if something happens to you? What if you get killed and I never get the chance...," I say, but he interrupts me.

He slams his lips down onto mine, taking me in a kiss that leaves any other kiss I have ever had in shame. He wraps his arms around my middle, picking me up. I have no choice but to wrap my legs around his waist. He continues kissing me as he walks over and sits down on the bench, with me now straddling him.

Our tongues dual as we kiss each other as if our lives depend on it. And in a sense, they do. I don't want to lose him just as he doesn't want to lose me. Neither of us would survive. We are two parts to one soul. I had never believed in soul mates. I thought it was something that people made up to convince themselves that they chose the right person. But sitting here, kissing Cooper, feeling... well, feeling everything, I know that he is my other half.

He puts his hands in my hair, tilts my head, and deepens the kiss. I don't ever want this to end. There is moaning. I couldn't tell you if it was him or me, but who cares. He nips at my lips, then kisses along my jaw and down my neck. He buries his face in my neck, occasionally kissing and nipping at my skin. I have my hands around his neck. It's as if we are one. There is no space between us.

He finally pulls back and rests his forehead against mine.

"You have no idea how long I have waited to do that," he says quietly.

"I think I do," I say back.

We both laugh softly.

"I will save your brother. And I will always come back to you. Always," he says with so much promise that there is no room for doubt of any kind.

"And I will stay safe. You know, I'm not only going so that I can be there for Austin," I say. "I'm going to make sure that you come back to me."

This earns me another kiss. This one is even better than the first.

18

Rescue Time

" Promise me that you'll come back to me," I say as we are lying in bed that night, wrapped in each other's arms.

We spend the night just holding each other. I'm pretty sure we each dozed off and on a little bit, but neither of us wanted to miss a moment of this time together.

It's morning now, the morning of the rescue, and I am nervous. No, not nervous... scared. I'm scared that something is going to happen and I'm going to lose both of them.

"Baby, nothing in heaven or hell is going to keep me from you," he says, kissing my nose.

I lean up to look into his eyes.

"I'm not kidding, Coop. Swear to me that everything is going to be ok. That both you and Austin are going to come back to me."

He cups both of my cheeks and pulls me down into a deep kiss. Within seconds, we are desperate. He pulls me so that I am straddling him. This takes the kiss to an entirely new level. When he finally pulls back and looks at me, there is a tear running down his cheek.

I reach up and wipe it away.

"Cassidy Daniels, I promise you that we will be together again. I am never letting you go. You mean the world to me. I love you with all my heart and I intend to spend the rest of my life with you. Even if that means I have to spend the rest of my life chasing you around, trying to convince you of your love for me," he says in all seriousness.

"I'm going to hold you to that, Cooper Matthews."

I lean down and rest my head on his chest, completely laying on top of him. He wraps his arms around me and runs his fingers up and down my back.

We stay like that until his alarm goes off, signaling the end of our time together, at least for now.

Somberly, we both get up and get dressed. If I'm not mistaken, we are both moving on the slow side, not wanting this moment to end. But unfortunately, time is an evil bitch.

The phone in the room rings.

"Matthews," Cooper answers. He's quiet, listening to whoever is on the other end. His face gives nothing away. Eventually, he hangs up.

"They are moving up the timeline. We leave in thirty," he says. "They fear that the facility may have been tipped off."

"Then maybe we should hold off, and try another day."

"No Cass. If we don't do this today, we lose our chance. They will know that they got the better of us. It has to be today."

He comes over to me and pulls me into his arms.

"I love you," he tells me.

I want to say it. I do. But something holds me back. Fear of losing him, fear of being alone, I can't say.

He holds me just a moment longer, then squeezes me before stepping back. He takes my hand, and together, we go to face what the day holds.

• • • •

The time is here, and I am fighting the tears, trying to appear calm. There is a line of vehicles, all stocked to the rim with weapons and explosives. The chipmunks are in the first vehicles, as they are taking a slightly different route. They are to get there first, to set up the charges. They have an hour to complete their task.

Then, the guys on the ground will advance. The signal to advance is the first explosion. The timing is exact for these guys. I don't know the specific plans once they enter the building, Cooper wouldn't tell me out of fear of scaring me. The only thing I know is that from start to finish, the whole thing should only take twenty-five minutes.

Their man on the inside, Ziggy, is to start a riot. From what I heard, he has a few of the guys that he trusts who will help with that so that he is not implicated. Once he hears the first explosion, he is to gather the ones we are bringing back with us and head to the extraction point.

Gunner and I are in the last vehicle. We aren't following them the entire way. We are headed to a holding area. Everyone has communication pieces and they have given Gunner and me a radio to listen in on everything happening. We won't be able to see what is going on, but we can listen to it. We are both armed. Cooper convinced the General of my training. He insisted on seeing me handle the weapon so we took him to the shooting range, to prove that I can shoot. He was impressed, mumbling something about being able to use me in the future. I don't think Cooper heard that, or he probably would have had something to say about it.

Gunner is in the driver's seat, and I am just about to get in the passenger's side when someone grabs me from behind.

"Promise me again that you'll be safe," he says in my ear, holding me tightly.

I turn in his arms and pull him down for a kiss. It's not an overly passionate kiss, but it's exactly what we both need. When I pull back, I look into his eyes.

"I'll promise, if you will, too," I say.

He pulls me into a hug. He squeezes me tight, but I don't complain. I'm trying not to think about the fact that this could be the last time that I see him. But it's in the back of my mind. I'm sure he is thinking the same thing.

"You know what?" I ask him.

"What, babe."

"I want a back rub tonight when we get back," I say, a tear slipping free.

He wipes the tear away and lightly rubs his lips against mine.

"You got it," he says.

He helps me get into my seat and buckles my seat belt.

"I have your word, Private," he reminds Gunner.

"On my life, sir," Gunner says.

Cooper nods at him. He looks at me and smirks.

"Until tonight," he says and winks, then walks away.

I watch him until he is out of my sight.

"He'll be ok, Cass. The only guy better than him is your brother," he says, trying to reassure me.

Within minutes, the General comes out and everyone falls silent and turns their eyes to the man in charge.

"Keep it tight and have each other's backs. I don't care if you are Army, Marine, or just a citizen of this great country. You are here because you care. Go there and bring our boys back to us." He pauses, looking around. His eyes find mine and he seems to decide something. "I want you all to remember that you are taking a viable female with you." I cringe at that word. I hate that word. "She may not be in on the mission, but she must be protected at all costs," he says, staring directly at Gunner. Talk about pressure. "I don't care what happens. She cannot be taken. Go. Go and make me proud."

"Oorah," someone calls out, and all the Marines call out the same.

The vehicles all start and my stomach drops. This is it.

I have never prayed before, but I find myself sending up a silent prayer.

"Please, don't let me lose them."

I feel like I have been sitting here for days. In reality, I think it has been only fifteen minutes. We are sitting in a field, just behind a wall of tall trees facing the facility. The boys all left their vehicles here and headed off on foot. Cooper gave me a wink before he turned around and led the men away. We are at the rally point. If anyone gets injured or separated, this is where they will come. This is also where they will meet up when the mission is complete.

All I can think about is what Cooper is doing. Is he thinking about me? Part of me hopes that he is, but the other part is hoping that he isn't, that he is focusing on the task at hand.

"Everything will be fine, Cassidy," Gunner says for about the fiftieth time. I look over at him and smile wanly. "Look, I know you don't want to hear it, but these men, this is what they do. They have been doing this for years. Years, Cassidy. They won't fail. They don't know how to," he says, which does make me feel better.

I hadn't thought of it that way. These are military men, and this is a mission. They spend their lives training for this. I have no right to doubt them. But that doesn't mean that I can't worry.

"Thank you, Gunner. But I am still scared," I say.

He takes my hand and squeezes it. He holds it for a few seconds then rips it away. It makes me laugh.

"Did I burn you?" I ask.

"Please, oh please don't tell him I touched you. He'll kill me," he says looking terrified.

I just laugh. "I won't tell him, I promise."

We sit in silence for what feels like forever. After an eternity, yes, I'm being dramatic, our radio comes to life.

"All right team. I need a go from everyone if you are ready and in position," it's Cooper. He's the lead on this mission.

"Team two, good to go," I hear Teddy say.

"Team four, good to go," another voice says.

"Team three, good to go," the last voice says.

There are extraction teams and the chipmunks.

"Command team, good to go," Cooper says.

It's a relief to hear his voice.

The next few minutes are silent. Then, the first explosion goes off. We are far enough away that we can just make out the smoke over the tops of the trees. It was big enough to feel, though. The Jeep shook slightly.

Then, it's go-time. Cooper is shouting commands as he advances.

"Door left, door left," he shouts, which is followed by "clear!"

"Stairway right."

"Clear."

"Coop, straight ahead."

"North corridor, hostiles!"

"North corridor? Is that Cooper's location," I ask desperately.

"No. He's on the south side," Gunner says, listening intently to the radio.

Commands are being shouted. I can hear gunfire. No one speaks for a while, but we can hear the fighting. There is shouting and screaming.

"Over here," someone shouts.

I hear, what sounds like a metal door opening, and then a sound that makes me cry.

"Daniels, are you hurt?"

"No. I'm good. Give me a gun," Austin says firmly.

He's alive. I reach up and cup my hands over my mouth to keep from sobbing. I know they kept telling me that they knew he was ok, but hearing his voice, and having absolute confirmation is a little too much right now.

"This way."

"Look out!"

Gunfire, then a second explosion. Someone was really close to the explosion because it sounded like a roar through the radio.

"Report," Cooper says.

"Team three, we have Daniels."

"Team two, ready. All civilians accounted for."

"Team four, still fighting."

More screaming and fighting. Gunfire. And the final explosion.

A male groan is heard, loudly.

"Cooper, get up!"

I sit forward on my seat.

"Cooper," I shout.

"Coop, let's go. Check his pulse," I hear someone say.

Did they mean Cooper's pulse? Oh my God, did he get hit, was it the explosion? I can't breathe. I think I am screaming because I feel Gunner grab my arms. I can see his mouth moving but I can't hear anything. A few minutes pass and I realize I could be missing information on Cooper. I shake my head and look at the radio. I must have stopped struggling because Gunner lets me go and turns his attention back to the radio.

There is more shouting, but no one else is talking about Cooper. I don't know if that means he is ok, or... I refuse to think that.

"Rally point, rally point!"

"Move, move, move, move, move!"

I look up in time to see someone break through the trees. I jump out of the Jeep and run over. It's Al, Teddy, and Simon. I run over to them. They see me coming and immediately throw their hands up.

"We haven't heard anything. We completed our part of the mission and headed back," Simon says.

I pace back and forth, waiting for anyone, anything. Gunner comes up holding the radio, but all I hear is heavy breathing. They are running.

Al, Simon, and Teddy come up and stand with me. They try and joke with me, telling me stories about Cooper and Austin. But I can't even tell you what they said. I need to see them. I need to know that they are ok.

About thirty minutes later, they start to trickle in. Because the teams were in different parts of the facility, some were further away than others and it will take them longer to get back. There are a few injured, but nothing terrible. A couple of gunshot wounds, some injured by shrapnel from the explosions. But no one was lost, that we know of anyway. After the first group has been treated by the medics, another group appears.

"Cass," I hear someone shout my name.

I turn and see Austin, and the next thing I know, I am in his arms. I don't know who ran at who, but it doesn't matter. He is holding me tightly and I am squeezing him back just as hard.

He eventually pulls back. "I can't believe you are here! What are you doing here? You should be back at the base!"

"Don't you shout at me! I am here because I want to be. I haven't seen you in months and that is the first thing you can say to me," I shout at him.

"I'm sorry, Cass. I'm so sorry I let us get separated. It was the only way I could save you. I'm just glad that Cooper found you. You have to tell me everything, but later. I need to see him. Is he back yet?"

I look around at the rest of the guys who have come back since we found each other. But I don't see him. I do see one of the guys that was on his team, so I run over to him.

"Gomez! Where is Coop?" He is limping pretty badly, possibly shot in the leg. I can't tell.

"He was right behind me," he says, looking around.

I look into the woods and don't see anyone else. The medics are making their rounds, working on the people they rescued, the soldiers, basically everyone. Our small rescue group has turned into a giant mob of activity.

About fifteen minutes have passed and no Cooper. No anyone else either. It appears that every one that is returning is back.

I start to cry.

Austin must see me because he comes over and pulls me into his arms.

"What is it, Cass? What happened? Are you hurt?" he asks, shouting out question after question, pulling back to examine me. He checks me from head to toe, looking for injuries.

"I didn't get to tell him," I say quietly between sobs.

"Didn't get to tell who what, Cass?" he asks, confused.

I just stand there in my brother's arms, sobbing. I can't believe I let my fear keep me from telling Cooper that I love him. He died, not knowing. He died rescuing my brother for me, and I didn't have the courage to admit it. I will never forgive myself. He was the best thing that ever happened to me. He protected me. He took care of me. He was everything. And I was so stupid.

Time passes slowly. Austin tries to get me to talk to him, but I can't find any words. I should tell him that I was in love with his best friend. That it's my fault he is dead. He pushed this mission forward because he knew that I needed my brother. He sacrificed himself, as he always has, for my happiness. Little did he know that any chance of happiness that I had in life, died with him.

Austin leaves me sitting on the edge of one of the trucks so that he can help with the wounded. Ten men went in, and they came back with over forty. A successful mission. Except they lost the best of them. I don't think Austin is thinking about it. As much as this hurts me, I have to remember that he was Austin's best friend.

After a few minutes, Austin gathers a few of the men by the edge of the forest. I hear them talking. They are planning to go back and look for Cooper. No man left behind they say. There are five of them, consisting of Austin, the chipmunks, and Gomez, the guy from his team. They are loading up on weapons and supplies when there is a commotion by the forest.

There is a murmur amongst the men, and everyone begins to gather at the entrance to the forest.

I get up from the truck and make my way over, trying to see what is going on.

"It's Matthews," someone shouts.

I just about knock everyone over as I take off for the trail. I see him and can't stop myself from jumping on him. He sees me coming and catches me just as I jump at him. He picks me up and holds me close. I wrap my legs around his waist and sob.

He pulls back to kiss me. It's frantic and messy, but I really don't care. He's alive.

"I love you, Cooper Matthews! I love you, so much! Don't ever leave me again!"

I say this between kisses. I kiss his face, his neck, pretty much anywhere I can get my mouth. When I finally stop crying, he pulls back to look at me. He's dirty, and bloody, with cuts on his face and arms, but as far as I can see, he is ok.

He smirks. "I knew I'd wear you down."

I stick my tongue out at him which he quickly grabs with his teeth. This leads to another deep kiss.

Someone clears their throat behind us. Cooper doesn't drop me immediately. He slows the kiss, finally ending it with a kiss on my forehead. He puts me down and takes my hand. We turn, to see a scowling Austin staring at us with his arms crossed over his chest.

"Is there something you two want to tell me?" he asks, looking pissed.

Cooper walks over to him, completely ignoring what Austin said, and pulls him into a hug.

"It's so good to see you, brother," Cooper says, clapping him on the back.

Austin pulls away and just stares between the two of us.

"Well?" he asks again.

"Austin, I love your sister. I have loved her for a long time. Between you constantly talking about her and me listening to and watching your conversations with her, I fell in love. She means everything to me. I would never hurt her," Cooper says calmly, pulling me close.

Austin looks at me.

"And you? You feel the same?" he asks.

I walk over to Austin and grab his hand.

"I love him, Aus. He has protected me and taken care of me from the second we met. I owe him my life, just as you owe him yours. I want to be with him, forever," I say, looking back at Cooper, who winks at me.

Austin pulls me into a hug. "God, I've missed you, kid. I can't even tell you. If you're happy, and this is what you want, I can't imagine a better man to take care of you." He pulls back and looks at Cooper. "But you and I have a lot to talk about, man."

Cooper laughs and walks over to us. He pulls me into his arms, and I gladly melt into him. We grab Austin and pull him into the hug. The three of us just stand there, holding each other, for the longest time.

I have both of my men back.

20

Back to Reality

A successful mission. No casualties. Minor injuries. I guess it doesn't get much better than that. Except it does. I have my brother back. I got to tell Cooper that I love him, and we have the whole future in front of us.

We make it back to the base and there is a huge welcome party waiting for us. Cooper had reported the results of the mission back to the General via radio, so they knew we were coming and that we had company.

When he started his mission back at the beginning, the General had fifteen men with him. Now, having taken out five facilities, and rescued so many, the base is up to over two hundred people. They have picked up supplies along the way and a lot of the rescued are people with fighting experience and enough motivation to carry the whole place. There are policemen, military men, and people from the streets of this country. And all of them have one huge thing in common. They have lost their mothers, their wives, their daughters – people that they love.

We are in the cafeteria at the main building, and I am walking around just listening to the stories. There are stories of survival, of loss, of heartache. But everyone is coming together. The most common thing I hear, though, is that they want to keep the fight going. Everyone is on the same page, that we must keep taking down the facilities. We owe it to the people there, we owe it to those they lost. But most importantly, we owe it to those who can't fight for themselves.

I find a seat in the corner and just collapse. It has been the most emotionally and physically exhausting day. After a while, Austin spots me and sits down across from me.

"So, you and Coop?" he asks.

I smile. "Weird, right?" I ask.

"No. It's not actually. I have to admit that I pictured the two of you together. He's the best man I know. There's no one better for you," he says emphatically.

I feel someone place their hands on my shoulders and I smile. Cooper leans down and kisses my cheek.

"Are you ready to get some rest, baby?" he asks me.

"Ugh. Gross. Ok, so maybe this will take some time to get used to," Austin says, wrinkling his nose in disgust.

We all laugh. Cooper helps me stand, and I walk over and give Austin a hug.

"Promise me we'll talk tomorrow," I say. "I have missed you so much."

"Come get me when you are up," he says. "I'm pretty sure everyone is taking the day off tomorrow."

Austin and Cooper do a quick bro-hug.

"I owe you, man," Austin says to him. "I mean it. Not only did you save my ass, but you took care of Cass. I don't know that I could ever repay you."

"She saved me, too. I don't know what I'd do without her," Cooper says, pulling me close.

Austin nods and turns away. He makes it a few feet before a few of the men pull him down at their table. They begin to laugh and talk. It makes me smile.

"Shall we?" Cooper asks, guiding me towards the door.

We go out to the Jeep and head back over to our building. It is a silent ride, both of us reflecting on the events of the day. We get to our building and walk hand in hand inside. We wave at the guard and make our way to the room. He opens the door for me, and motions for me to enter. Once inside, everything hits me, and I lose it.

Before all this crap started, I never cried. I know you don't believe me, but it's true. I can't even tell you the last time I cried. But now, I feel like everything is so fragile. Things can change at the drop of a hat, and you never know what is going to happen.

Cooper pulls me into his arms, but I fight him.

"I thought I lost you today. I really thought you were gone," I say.

"I'm so sorry, baby. I fought like hell to get back to you, I really did. When the last explosion hit, I was too close. It knocked me on my ass. I was a little disoriented when I got up, so it was hard to run. I got separated from the men when we got outside," he says quickly, his words almost blending together.

"I'm just so glad you are ok. I realized when you were gone, that I was letting my fear control me. I was so afraid of losing another person I loved, I forgot that loving someone is what life is all about."

He pulls me back into him and holds me close. I realize at that moment, that this is my favorite place to be, in the arms of the man I love. We stand there holding each other, reveling in the feeling that we are both alive, and together.

Eventually, he pulls back to kiss me. It starts out slow but quickly builds.

He backs me towards the bed and gently lays me down. He climbs down on top of me, his hands on either side of my head. He leans down and nuzzles his nose against mine. It's sweet and intimate. Something only lovers share.

My heart is beating wildly. I'm sure he remembers, but I have never done this before.

"Coop," I say, but he stops me by putting his fingers over my mouth.

"I know, Cass. I know. If you want me to stop, you just have to say it. But I promise you, I'll make this perfect for you. You mean the world to me, and sharing this with you is... well, it's everything. I love you. I love you, so much. But I will wait if you want to," he says gently, caressing my face.

I don't even have to think about it.

"I want this, Cooper. I want you. I only want you, for the rest of my life. Maybe I shouldn't say that…," I say, but he cuts me off with a kiss. My heart is beating out of control. I have thought about this moment and what it would feel like for a long time. I had always hoped my first time would be with someone I loved. I just never expected it to be with the only man I will ever love. I know I haven't known him long, but it feels right between us. He might have the advantage here because he has technically known me longer, but I know his heart, and that is all that matters.

He sits back and pulls his shirt over his head. Holy. Shit. I know I have seen him shirtless before, but damn. I am a lucky woman.

I must blush because he chuckles.

"Like what you see? Oh wait, you made it clear back at the facility that you enjoy looking at me," he teases.

"Don't be that guy. Don't be the guy who is hot and knows it," I say.

He smiles as he leans down to kiss me. As he kisses me, he begins to remove my clothes. My sweatshirt comes off first, then my bra. My pants are last, leaving me in only my panties. He sits back on his heels and just looks at me. I begin to get self-conscious and try to cover myself. He grabs my hands, though, and smiles sweetly at me.

"You are the most beautiful woman I have ever seen. I am so lucky that you are mine," he says, pressing a kiss to my lips.

He trails kisses down my neck. I try to just take it all in and feel what he is doing to me. I don't want to forget this moment for the rest of my life. This feels big like I am giving a part of myself to him. From this point on, we are one. He is part of me.

Cooper is gentle and loving. Taking his time with me. He ignites my senses and sets me on fire. We make love for hours, all throughout the night. We spend time exploring each other, discovering what we enjoy the most. He now knows me better at this point than I probably know myself, and I him.

I am lost in him.

Afterward, with my head on his chest, I revel in the sound of his heart. It means he is alive, and here with me. It is very humbling to realize that the person you love, loves you back, probably even more if you listen to him. He has gone above and beyond, the entire time that we have known each other, to prove that he would do anything for me. And he has proven that.

"What are you focusing on so hard? I can almost hear your mind going," he says, kissing the top of my head.

I look up at him and smile.

"Just that I am lucky to have you. You have been so strong, so protective. I know that I wouldn't be here if it weren't for you."

He pulls me down for a kiss. "I am only this way because of you. You make me want to be better. I want to be everything that you need. As cheesy as that sounds, it's true. I am completely in awe of you, and if we live to be a hundred, it still wouldn't give me enough time to love you," he says.

I fall asleep in the arms of the man I love. And I couldn't be happier.

• • • •

I wake up to kisses along my neck.

"Are you finally awake?" he asks in his deep, sexy morning voice.

"Mmmmm," I say sleepily. "Now this is the way to wake up."

"I promise to wake you up like this every day for the rest of our lives," he says, making his way up to nibble on my earlobe.

"You know, you keep saying things like that and I'm going to start believing them," I warn him.

He stops his maddening torture and pulls back to look at me.

"Cassidy, I meant every word that I said to you. I have loved you for years. I have wanted you for years. And now that I have you, I am never letting you go. I can't. If I could, I would go out right now a buy a ring so that I could propose to you. But unfortunately, that isn't in the cards right now."

I look at him, trying to determine if he is serious.

"You… you want to marry me?" I ask, shocked.

"Yes, more than anything. But for now, my priority is to make sure that you stay safe. The rest will have to wait."

He leans down and kisses me. We spend the morning in bed, cuddling, talking, and making love. I learn more about him this morning than I ever could just dating him. There is something so intimate about just holding each other while talking about your likes and dislikes, your hopes, and your dreams.

Eventually, we decide we have to get up and start the day. We agree that we should shower first which ends up taking a while because we end up together in the same stall. It wasn't my intention, but when he walked in naked, what was I supposed to do? I mean, really. The man is gorgeous, I couldn't say no.

We are now dressed and back in our room.

"What are you going to do while I am with Austin?" I ask him.

"I'm not sure. I know I have to catch up with the General at some point to fill him in on the mission. Maybe I will do that now so that I don't miss any time with you," he says, pulling me into his arms.

"No way, mister. I have to go get Austin. We are not starting this again or we will never get out of here," I say, trying my best to keep him at arms' length.

"Is that really such a bad thing?" he asks, kissing me again.

I get distracted for a minute, but quickly snap back to reality when there is a knock on our door. I pull myself away from Cooper to answer it. I find a smiling Austin standing on the other side.

"I figured if I didn't come and get you, you would never be able to drag yourself out of bed," he says with a hint of menace in his voice.

I blush. "Uh, we just woke up," I say.

"Uh, huh. Right," he says, smirking.

He walks over and punches Cooper in the arm. "Why don't we meet up for lunch in an hour?" Cooper suggests.

"Oh, what's the matter buddy? Can't survive without my sister for longer than a few minutes," Austin says, teasing Cooper.

"As a matter of fact, no. I can't survive without her," he says, winking at me.

"Come on, kid. Let's go, before this caveman beats me up and drags you away by your hair," Austin says.

We are halfway down the hall before Cooper catches us to give me one last kiss. I just smile and shake my head at him.

Austin and I decide that we want to sit outside and enjoy the sun, so we head over to one of the picnic areas and sit at a table. There is a slight breeze, but the sun is strong today, shining bright. I hope it is a sign of things to come.

"So, in all seriousness, kid. Are you ok?"

"I'm fine, Aus. It hasn't been the best few months of my life, but I'm a tough cookie," I say.

He grabs my hands. "Tell me. What happened after we got separated," he asks.

So, I do. I tell him everything. How I got picked up, the experiments, the torture, the presentation, the fight. As if that isn't enough, I explain how it was in the facility with Cooper. He gets angry when I describe how he acted towards me, but I after I fill him in on Cooper's story, he said he doesn't like it, but he understands. We talk about the escape and the cave. We never keep secrets, so I tell him about how I felt during all of this. How I was falling for Cooper, but everything was just so messed up. He asks questions here and there, but mostly just lets me get it all out. When I finish, he is silent.

"Say something," I say quietly, not able to look at him yet. When I do, he looks angry. But I can't tell who it is directed at.

"Honestly?" he asks.

"Always," I say. "I always want you to be honest with me."

"I'm pissed, Cass! Pissed that you had to go through any of that. You were tortured! You were beaten! I mean, seriously, how are you sitting here telling me all of this and not falling apart?"

I think about that for a second. It doesn't take long for me to be able to answer him.

"It's Cooper, Aus. He was there, every step of the way. He might not have been there when I was being tortured or beaten, but he was there to help me heal from it and to protect me the rest of the way. I'm not going to lie, I thought I was broken. When I lost you, when I thought you were dead," I choke up a bit and have to pause for a second. "I had no idea how I was going to go on. I mean, losing mom and then dad was more than enough, but to lose you, too... I can't even describe it. I needed something, someone to be there for me. And even though he couldn't talk to me at first, Cooper was there. It was all the little things he did. Like making sure I was in the bed every night and sitting with me on the floor when I just needed to cry. He's a good man, Aus. Almost as good as you."

He pulls me in for a hug. We just sit there, holding each other. It feels so good to have him back in my arms.

"I never thought I would get to hug you again, Aus," I say, wiping a tear away.

"I'm here, kid. I told you I would find you again. Don't doubt the love of a big brother," he says.

"Best friend, too," I add with a smile. "So, what happened with you?"

He groans. "It's not a pretty story, Cass. Let's just say I made it through and call it a day."

"No way! I had to spill my guts. Don't pull this big brother crap and try to protect me. With everything going on, you owe it to me to tell me," I say with a growl.

He puts his head down and shakes it.

"Don't say I didn't warn you," he says.

"When they first picked me up, I was thrown into the back of a truck with several other men. All of them in various stages of consciousness. All of us though were injured. I had my gunshot wound. Another guy's head was split open, and he was covered in blood. It was gruesome. It felt like we traveled for hours. I honestly couldn't tell you. I was in so much pain and fighting to stay awake. I was afraid of what they would do to me if I fell asleep.

"When we got to the facility, they put us all in a large, plain room. One by one, we were called out. I was one of the last to go. We didn't talk to each other, afraid that someone might be listening. When they called me, I was taken to a medical room where they worked on my arm. Thankfully, the bullet went right through, so it just had to be cleaned and stitched. Not the worst wound I've ever had, so it was bearable," he says.

"What do you mean "not the worst wound you've had?" You never told me you were injured before," I say accusingly.

He looks at me sheepishly but then continues.

"Uh, so anyway. Once I was treated, they took me to shower and clean myself up. I agree with you, that even though I was under less-than-stellar circumstances, that was one of the best showers I ever had. After not having showered for months, it felt so good."

We laugh. It's amazing how your priorities change when you are living through the end of society.

"I was then taken to see the head doctor in the facility. He told me his name was Dr. Carpenter. He explained he needed to draw some blood and collect some... uh... other types of samples to test my ability to reproduce."

I cringe at this, trying not to imagine them collecting the "other" samples.

"Once everything was finished, they began the interrogation. I was asked everything and anything, probably the same as you. They left me alone in the room for hours, if not days. I guess they finally determined that I was a good bet and they put me into the general population of breeders. I had my own cell, but apparently, there is a pecking order in those facilities. One guy, who was the self-proclaimed alpha of the group, had people challenging me daily. I was fighting every day. I had to watch my back everywhere I went. There was always someone watching me, ready to jump if I was distracted. I had to constantly be on my toes, eyes in the back of my head and all that."

He goes on, to describe a few of the fights. I get lost in his tale, picturing everything that he went through. Suddenly, it occurs to me that I never once asked Cooper what it was like for him. I am a terrible person.

"After a few weeks, I was approached by Ziggy, the General's man on the inside. He would come to me at night, and we would talk. I asked what kinds of connections he had, hoping like hell he would be able to get me some kind of information on you. It took days to send a message to the General and then get a response. It was absolute torture. I eventually heard that you were in a facility, but that Cooper was with you and taking care of you. Then, word came that you both escaped and were planning the attack to take down my facility. And well, I think you know the rest."

I sit in silence. This entire world is extremely fucked up. No one is safe. No one. This morning, all I could think about was living my happily ever after with Cooper. Now, after hearing what Austin went through, and pairing that with what I went through, all I can think about it fighting back.

"We have to keep going," I say adamantly.

"Absolutely. But what do you mean, we?" he asks.

"I mean, all of us. Anyone who is willing and able. We have to keep taking down these facilities. We can't keep letting people go through this. The women, the men, the kids. The government is out of control, and we have to do something!"

"That's the plan, Cass, but to be perfectly honest, you are not going anywhere. Your fight is here, helping on the base. Let us do the fighting. I don't want you hurt," he says, grabbing my shoulders and forcing me to look at him. I am struggling to get away.

"No, Austin! No. I am part of this fight, whether you like it or not. I cannot just sit here and wait while you and Cooper go out and risk your lives. I was there, Aus. I saw what they do. I have to help. You trained me. If it wasn't for this, then why? No, I need to help. Please don't just push me aside like some little kid. This is it. Don't you get it?" I plead my case, hoping that he sees my point.

He sighs and turns away from me.

"Hey, guys. What's up?" Cooper says, walking up. He slows as he sees both of our faces. "What's going on?"

"Austin is trying to tell me that I have to stay at the base when you guys go out to take down more facilities. Tell him I'm coming, Coop. Go on, tell him," I say.

Cooper looks back and forth between Austin and me. He and Austin seem to have a silent conversation before Cooper looks back at me.

His face settles into that of someone who is about to deliver bad news.

"No! No! Don't you dare," I warn him.

"Cass," he starts, but I cut him off.

"Don't. Just don't!" I say, completely defeated. "Had I known that you two were going to gang up on me, I wouldn't have let this happen," I say, pointing between me and Cooper.

I instantly regret saying that with the look on Cooper's face. But honestly, I am so angry right now, I just can't find it in myself to care.

"You know what? You two just go ahead and fight all my battles for me. I'll go and hide in the closet. Let me know when you want me to have dinner ready for you and don't forget to leave me your dirty clothes so that I can wash them. I'll just be the good little girl that you want."

I turn and storm away, leaving them both staring after me. Yeah, yeah. I know. That was totally childish, and I just threw a temper tantrum. But what was I supposed to do? They think I can't take care of myself.

Well, I'll show them.

21

Dejected

I make my way over to the Administration building, intent on seeing General McConnell. I hope if I plead my case to him, he will allow me to go on future rescue missions. He was definitely impressed with my ability to handle a weapon. I'm sure he will find something for me to do.

Once inside, I bypass the security guard and head down the hallway to his office. His assistant sees me coming.

"Hello, Miss Daniels. Is there something I can help you with?" she asks, politely.

"I would like to see the General, please. If he's available," I say.

"I'm sorry, dear. He's in a meeting. I can schedule you an appointment to meet with him tomorrow if you'd like."

Of course, he's busy. Of course. "No, thank you. I'll just speak with him another time."

I turn and make my way out of the building. I'm not sure what to do at this point so I just head back to the room. I stop in the common area on our floor and curl up on the window seat, pull my knees up to my chest, and stare out the window.

Everything has changed. Everything. Normal life no longer exists. This, whatever this is, is the new normal. Am I an endangered species? Is that what I should consider myself? No, that's wrong. I am viable – and if it's possible, I think the word like it is disgusting, not worthy of even thinking. That's what they called me. That's all that matters. Because I can have babies for them, that is my value. It's all I am good for. At least, that's how it feels.

Everyone is fighting for their lives. Or just, fighting for life, in general. The remaining women, and girls, need to be protected. I think of Shelby, sitting at that facility, just waiting for them to begin their experiments on her. She's young, so we have some time, but I'll be damned if I sit back and allow that to happen. I can't let her go through that. She is such a sweet and innocent soul. It would break her.

I realize that I have been sitting here for a while, feeling sorry for myself. I hate this feeling. I know I should be willing to do anything to help, but I just want to be out there, on the front lines, so to speak. I know I can be of help. I may not be a soldier, but I think that after everything that I have gone through, there has to be something that I can do.

I take a step back and try to see it from the boys' perspective. They are just trying to keep me safe. I know that. But I can't help but feel dismissed, dejected. I know I can help out there. I don't just want to sit around and wait. That's not who I am. I am a fighter. I know you probably don't believe me because of all the crying I've done. But I really am a fighter. I stand up for what I believe in.

I don't know how long I have been sitting here. I eventually hear the door to the stairway open. I can hear Austin and Cooper talking in the hallway.

"This is the only other place she could be," Cooper says.

"Now just wait, Coop. We can't just go storming in there telling her she can't fight with us. She's more than capable and you know it. The problem is us. We want to protect her," Austin says, trying to reason with Cooper.

"I know, man, I know. But every time I even think about her being out there, where she could get hurt... it kills me. I can't risk losing her, man. I just got her," Cooper explains sounding frantic.

"You think I want her hurt?" Austin asks.

"Of course, not. But that's different. She's your sister, man. She's my everything. My world," Cooper says.

I smile at this. He's never been one to hide his feelings from me. But I honestly thought he would just be like that with me. To hear him tell Austin makes me feel so lucky. He really is the perfect man.

They talk for a few more minutes before heading down the hallway. When they get to the doorway of the common room, Cooper glances my way and then does a double take. He strides right for me, scooping me out of the seat and holding me in his arms.

"Baby, I've been so worried," he says into my hair.

I just let him hold me for a minute, needing his comfort. I eventually pull back and look at both him and Austin.

"I'm sorry, guys. I was an idiot to throw a tantrum like that. I just felt like you were dismissing me without hearing what I was saying. I just want to help. And sitting here at the base is not enough." I try desperately to explain how I'm feeling. "It's like everything that I have seen, everything that I went through is nothing."

"That's not it at all, Cass. It's because of those things that you went through that we want to keep you safe. Neither of us can imagine you having to go through any of that again," Austin explains.

"I get it, I do. I know you both want me safe. But the fact is, as a... viable female," I spit the word, "I might be able to help out in different ways," I say.

They both think about that for a minute.

"Listen, nothing is planned at the moment. Let's just take some time to think about everything. The next time we plan a mission, we will include you," Cooper tells me.

My eyes must light up. He stops me before I can say anything.

"I'm not saying that you will be on the front lines. I'm just saying we will be open to suggestions," he says.

I can't complain about that. They are at least willing to consider it.

"Thank you," I say, wrapping my arms around his waist. "Thank you both."

22

The Next Steps

The next few days go by in a blur. Everyone is still healing from the last mission. It takes a while to get the new people set up in living quarters. Cooper and I spend a lot of time together, whether it be just hanging out in our room, or walking the base. It's just something that we both needed.

Austin spends a lot of time with the General. He tells me they are just going over the information that he has from the facility, but I feel like there is more to it.

The General calls a meeting and asks that I attend. Cooper and Austin had already received their invites, so I just assumed it was a military thing. But about an hour before it was to start, I got a message saying that the General would personally like me there. I can tell that the boys aren't happy about it, but after the discussion the other day, they say nothing.

We head over together, wanting to get there early.

"Cass, I know you were personally invited by the General, but please just sit back and listen. There is a certain behavior expected of us and I don't want you to inadvertently disrespect anyone. Unintentionally, of course," Austin says.

"I know how to behave in public, Aus. Geez. You act like I am an idiot. I know you big, strong, military guys are all respectful and everything. I'll just sit back and listen," I say, punching him in the gut, which earns me a swipe across the head.

"Now, now children," Cooper says. "We all need to be on our best behavior."

We make our way into the building and down the hall to the General's meeting room. We walk in to find not only our men, but several others that I do not recognize, but apparently, the boys do. They immediately stand at attention. I, of course, do nothing.

"Ah, Staff Sergeant Daniels. Staff Sergeant Matthews. I'd like you to meet Colonel Steven Walters," the General says.

"It is an honor to meet you, sir," Cooper says.

"At ease, gentlemen. I have heard great things about the both of you," Colonel Walters says, shaking each of their hands. "And who is this lovely young lady?"

Cooper wraps his arm around my shoulder and pulls me close. "This is Cassidy Daniels, my fiancé." Austin whips his head to the side at this revelation and stares at the two of us.

"I hadn't heard about the engagement. Congratulations, you two," General McConnell says.

"Me either," I grumble.

I step forward, shrugging out from underneath Cooper's arm, and extend my hand to the Colonel. "It's very nice to meet you, sir. I am Austin's sister," I say, letting Cooper know that I am not thrilled about the whole surprise engagement thing. He shakes my hand, firmly, as expected.

We all separate and head toward our seats.

"So, who is this guy?" I ask quietly.

"So, we aren't talking about you two getting married? Ok, then," Austin says sharply.

"Colonel Walters is legendary. He worked directly with the President as one of his advisers. Everyone in the Military has heard of him and his accomplishments."

Cooper pulls me to the side, away from Austin. "I'm sorry. It just kind of slipped out."

"Listen, Coop. I love you. I want to be with you. But we are a team. You don't get to make decisions for me. Are we clear?"

Austin must hear me because I see him smirking out of the corner of my eye.

"Yes, ma'am," Cooper says. "But I will marry you."

"Come on, Romeo. Let's find our seats," I say, pulling him back towards the table.

We all find our seats. General McConnell introduces Colonel Walters immediately.

"We are thrilled that he has decided to join us here," the General states.

Colonel Walters stands and addresses the room. "I have heard many things of your actions here at the base. Everything that you have done is extraordinary. As many of you know, I do not always agree with the President's actions, and as of late, I have been finding myself more and more disappointed in his plans. When I heard of your missions, I knew that I needed to help," he says. He pauses for a moment. I don't know this man, but anyone can recognize the look of a man who has known loss. "I lost my wife, Barbara, back in the beginning. It wasn't until a few weeks after the initial reports came in, so we thought she was safe. They called it the second wave. And it took her from me," he pauses again. "Our two boys are stationed overseas right now. They didn't get the chance to say goodbye."

Everyone is silent. No one knows what to do. He looks like a lost little boy standing up there. Something tells me that he does not open up often, and now that he has, we are all just sitting here staring at the poor man.

I get up and make my way over to him. I feel Cooper try to grab my hand, but I pull away. I walk right up to him and wrap my arms around him, pulling him into a hug. To say that the entire room is shocked is an understatement. I can see all their faces as I hug this poor, lost man, and I have to look away. If I keep looking at them, I will laugh.

It takes a second, but he wraps his arms around my shoulders and hunches in on me. I stand there consoling this man for several moments. He eventually pulls back and blinks a few times. I don't think this man has had a hug in a long time.

"Thank you, Miss Daniels," he says gruffly.

"You're welcome," I say quietly and make my way back to my seat. When I get there, Cooper leans over and kisses me on the cheek. "You are amazing, you know that?" he says. I just smile at him and take his hand.

The Colonel clears his throat. "That is exactly what we need right now. We need to support each other in these uncertain times. Which is why I'm here. I realized that everything that we are doing in those facilities is unethical. Yes, we have the responsibility of ensuring our survival. But not by hurting and researching on our own. I got word that the President is planning on expanding his research facilities. We cannot allow that to happen! What you have been doing here... well, we need to continue that work. We need to bring down as many facilities as we can."

There is a murmur of approval. The General gets up and continues the meeting. They have identified several more facilities and have infiltrated them by placing our own men in positions in those facilities. It will take time, but we will take them down.

"In conclusion, there is one vital piece of information that I haven't shared," the General says.

He looks over at me, sadly.

"The facility where Miss Daniels and Staff Sergeant Matthews were found... well, that is their headquarters. It is run by Dr. Garret Anderson, who reports directly to the President. All other facilities report to Anderson with their findings. They have the most staff, the most manpower, and the most weapons protecting that facility. When we get there, we must be willing to go above and beyond what it takes to destroy that facility."

I had an idea that Anderson was in charge, just by his cockiness and arrogance. But I am humble enough to admit that the thought of going back there terrifies me.

I must miss the General dismissing the meeting because I am still sitting there, stunned when everyone gets up to leave. Cooper sees me and sits back down.

"Talk to me, Cass."

"I mean, I'm not stupid. I knew we would have to go back there at some point. But to hear that he's in charge, that he is calling the shots... it scares the shit out of me," I say.

"You don't have to go back there, Cass. I don't want you anywhere near that man again. In fact, I want to be the one to put the bullet in his head when it comes time to do it. I won't let him get away with what he did to you."

I don't want to focus on that right now. I don't anyone else to die because of me. I stand up and make my way toward the door.

"Miss Daniels," I hear the General say behind me.

I turn to face him. "Yes, General," I start, but then see his face. "Yes, Mike."

He smiles. "I was hoping you would be willing to meet with the Colonel and I at some point to go over the details of your time with Dr. Anderson. Any little bit of information that you can provide will be helpful," he says.

I swallow. Cooper must have heard because he comes over to stand with us.

"General, she has been through enough. Do we really need to put her through it again?" he asks.

"No. No, it's fine. I want to help. Of course, Mike. Just let me know when you want me and I will be here," I say, trying to smile to hide my fear.

We say our goodbyes and make our way out of the building. Once outside, Cooper stops me.

"You don't have to do this, Cass."

I pull him down for a gentle kiss.

"Yes. I do, Cooper. I owe it to everyone we left behind in that facility. I owe it to Shelby. I promised her I would come back for her, and I intend to keep that promise. I will get her out of there," I vow.

"Just promise me that no matter what happens, we do this together," he says, narrowing his eyes at me.

I stare into his eyes, into the eyes of the man I love, and realize that no matter what happens, we will win this fight together.

"Of course," I say. "Of course."

As I sit here, staring at Mike and the Colonel, I am at a loss for words. It is a few days after the meeting, and they sent for me. They asked me to come alone, no Cooper. He was, of course, upset, but he can't challenge the requests of such high-ranking officers.

They have just finished asking me all the questions about my time with Dr. Anderson and then dropped a bomb on me.

"What do you think, Cassidy? Is that something you are willing to do for us? I think it is the best way for us to take him down," Mike says.

"It is completely up to you. But until you decide, please do not discuss this with anyone outside of this room. This is completely classified. We know you aren't military, but we hope that you will respect our request," the Colonel adds.

I just sit there, staring at them. What they are asking, what they want of me... I just don't know if I have it in me.

"I will need some time to think about it," I say quietly.

"Of course, Cassidy. Whatever you need. The plan can begin whenever you are ready. We have some time," Mike says, trying to reassure me.

I say my goodbyes and leave the office. Once the door is closed, I can hear them talking, probably about whether or not they think I will do what they have asked of me.

"Are you all right, dear?" Mike's secretary asks me. I walk past her desk in a daze. I think I manage to nod at her because she does not push to ask me any further questions.

I head outside and sit down on a bench. I don't want to go back to Cooper yet. I don't know how I am going to keep this from him, or Austin for that matter.

I look around. The base is now bustling with life. With all the people they have managed to bring back from the facilities, it is like a community. I can see families enjoying each other. They are the lucky ones. There are also groups of friends just walking around. A few people playing basketball over at the court between buildings. It almost appears, normal.

Life goes on, right? It makes me happy. I wish I could say that it makes me forget about what we just discussed. I know exactly how Cooper and Austin would react. They would flip. That's why I can't tell them.

I have to make this decision on my own.

A decision that could very well end my life.

But it would be for the greater good, as they said.

It would save thousands, if not more.

A sacrifice for a win.

Can I do this for everyone?

Can I make this sacrifice?

Can I find it in myself to go back in – as a viable female... with Dr. Anderson?

Thank you for reading my book. Please consider leaving a review. Independent authors like me depend on those reviews to spread the word.

Check out my website at www.wendyzuccauthor.com[1].

You can always reach me at wendyzuccauthor@gmail.com.

---

1. http://www.wendyzuccauthor.com

Don't miss out!

Visit the website below and you can sign up to receive emails whenever Wendy Zuccarello publishes a new book. There's no charge and no obligation.

https://books2read.com/r/B-A-TRVU-XJDFC

BOOKS2READ

Connecting independent readers to independent writers.

Did you love *Viable*? Then you should read *Loudening Silence* by Wendy Zuccarello!

Ashlyn Ford is deaf and alone in a world where even the strongest perish, and she has been deemed a traitor in her secluded, cult-like, fenced-in community. Her own father is out to kill her to protect his misguided dreams for control as Ashlyn has stolen his journal that could bring to light his sinister intentions.

When Ashlyn meets a Robin Hood-like Eli Sanders and his group of rebels from beyond the fences, she discovers acceptance and a newfound reason to challenge her father's abuse and diabolical goals. Aside from her parents, Eli and his group are the first people she has encountered that know ASL.

He and his brother Reed, who is also deaf, help Ashlyn understand the importance of trust and teach her that family can be found anywhere. The budding romance between Eli and Ashlyn is the fuel in their fight against her father.

In their efforts to protect their home and their future, Ashlyn and Eli discover that there is so much more to Ashlyn's past than they ever expected.

Ashlyn must fight the rage that consumes her every thought to protect those she has come to love. The future is uncertain, but she and Eli are determined to survive together.

Read more at https://www.wendyzuccauthor.com/.

Also by Wendy Zuccarello

All in Due Time
Winter Must End
Guarding Gwyn
Silent Hero
Sacrifice
Viable
Chasing Freedom
The Only Time We Get
Loudening Silence

Watch for more at https://www.wendyzuccauthor.com/.

About the Author

Wendy Zuccarello lives in central New Jersey with her husband, two teenagers, and many pets. She has her MFA in Creative Writing. In her spare time, when she is not reading or writing, she enjoys watching movies with her family, photography, and baseball.

Read more at https://www.wendyzuccauthor.com/.